An Element Of Truth

Twenty-Two Tales Of Two Tree Island

By Brian MacDonald

Sponsored by The Lions Club of Castle Point

Scribe Press

An Element Of Truth

© 2005 by Brian MacDonald

Published by Scribe Press
36 Burlington Gardens
Hadleigh, Essex SS7 2JL

ISBN: 0-9549648-0-2

Printed and bound by 4Edge Ltd
7a Eldon Way, Eldon Way Industrial Estate,
Hockley, Essex SS5 4AD
Telephone 01702 200243

For Ada & Angus and Rene & Fred

Fondest Memories

There is no end - merely a transition
From one existence to another.
We all live on in the memories of those who remain,
And our shadows are remembered
By those who knew us
And who fondly pass on our essence to others.

The enormity of the tragedy arising from the Asian Tsunami devastation in December 2004 reminds us that we are fortunate to live in a part of the world unaffected by these sort of disasters.

Production of this book has been sponsored by the Lions Club of Castle Point. All profits will be passed to the Lions Clubs International Foundation and applied to the relief of victims of the Asian Tsunami disaster.

We Serve

About The Author

Brian MacDonald was born in 1944 and spent his working life in the shipping industry, spending much time abroad and sometimes at sea. His interests are ancient history, music and poetry. He is author or editor of various non-fiction publications and articles and is a published poet. Brian is also the local Community Correspondent for one of his local newspapers. Married to Joan, with two grown-up sons, Brian has retired but is actively engaged in a variety of voluntary works.

While walking his dogs over the years, Brian has observed the development of Two Tree Island in Essex and some of the things he has seen have inspired this collection of twenty-two fictional short stories.

Brian's previous works include:

Non-Fiction:

I Remember ... [Editor]	Garden House Press (1987)
Dearest Mother [Editor]	Lloyds of London Press (1988)
The Landsmen's Lexicon [Editor]	Garden House Press (1988)
I Remember Too ... [Editor]	Garden House Press (1989)
Dearest Joan	Scribe Press (1993)
A Bedside Book	Forward Press (1999)
The *Unofficial* Guide To The Role & Duties Of An Appropriate Adult	Scribe Press (2004)
The Lions Club of Castle Point Recipe Collection [Editor]	Scribe Press (2004)

Poetry:

You Can See Why They Invented Paper	Scribe Press (1997)
Little Book of Poems I	Forward Press (1998)
Little Book of Poems II	Forward Press (1999)
Little Book of Poems III	Forward Press (2000)
Some Favourite Outpourings	Scribe Press (2004)
Monologues	Scribe Press (2004)

Contents

Two Tree Island

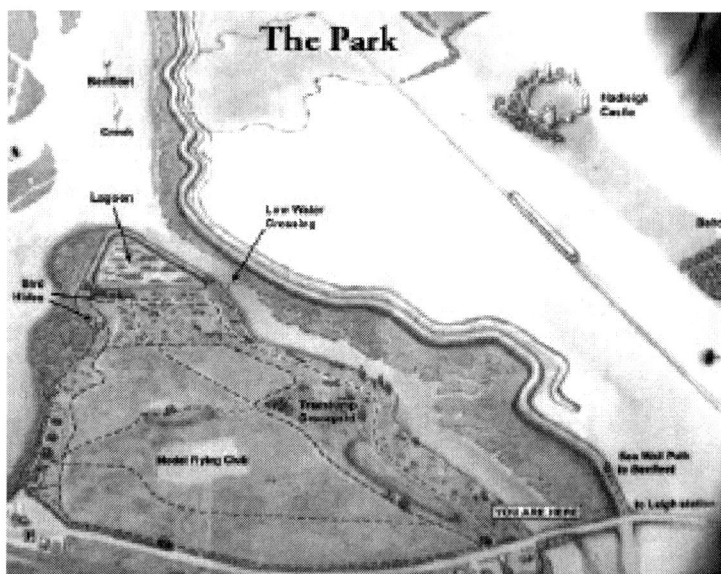

The Park

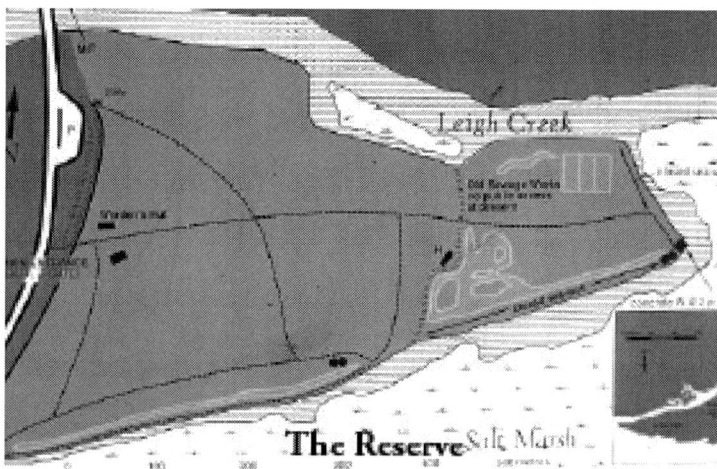

The Reserve

Introduction

This is a book about my favourite dog-walking place, Two Tree Island. [1]

The book is a blend of fact and fiction, a sort of literary *pot pourii*; there is something about my dogs in it, as well as something of me. There are some notes about the plant and wild life to be seen on the island throughout the year. But chiefly it is about the island itself and some of the things I have imagined might have happened on it.

Nestling behind Leigh-on-Sea Station in Essex is around one thousand acres of parkland and wildlife reserve with views over the Thames Estuary. Cross the railway bridge, stroll past the boat repair yard with the rigging of the boats snapping in the fresh breeze bearing a hint of ozone, pass along the sea wall for about half a mile, past the golf range and the motor boat club and then cross the little bridge over Leigh Creek.

You have arrived on Two Tree Island.

Surrounded by salt marsh, Two Tree Island is a lozenge-shaped piece of mainly reclaimed land, bounded by Leigh Creek to the north and Benfleet Creek to the south. Roughly divided into two halves, the eastern end of the island is a nature reserve and the western end a park. The island is a favourite haunt for many of us who live in this part of Essex and is an ever-changing haven of tranquillity, and sometimes the site of interesting and amusing events.

The island came into being in the 18th century when a sea wall was built round part of the salt marsh and the land thus enclosed was used for farming. Much more recently, part of it was used as a

---

[1] The wildlife reserve on the eastern side of Two Tree Island is managed by the Essex Wildlife Trust on behalf of Southend-on-Sea Borough Council. The western side of the island forms part of Hadleigh Castle Country Park and is managed by the Essex Ranger Service on behalf of a Joint Committee formed of representatives of Essex County Council, Southend-on-Sea Borough Council and Castle Point Borough Council.

rubbish tip and landfill site until this activity ceased in the 1970s and, later on, the rubbish was smoothed over and covered with topsoil and paths constructed.

There are now considerably more than two trees on Two Tree Island, though none of them are of any great age or height.

Nevertheless, the island attracts a great variety of trees and plants, small animals, birds and butterflies and, so it seems each autumn, a good proportion of the world's population of Brent Geese which come to rest from late September and noisily feed after their flight from their Siberian breeding-grounds.

There are decent views.

Hadleigh Castle, or what is left of this crumbling 13th century fortress atop the Hadleigh Downs, can be seen to the north, Leigh's 15th century St. Clement's Church with its distinctive watchtower guards the east, and Canvey Island and the coast of Kent squat to the south. To the east and south is the Thames Estuary in which are often seen a variety of deep sea ships passing Southend Pier, itself reputed to be the longest public pier in the world.

Two Tree is a favourite place for people to enjoy with their dogs, their children and friends; somewhere to have picnics, run or jog, cycle, bird-watch, fly kites or model aircraft or to sit and watch the ships passing up and down the Thames Estuary. For many of us, Two Tree Island is simply an ideal place in which to enjoy the peace and quiet that usually prevails there and a hour's escape from the noise and rush of life elsewhere.

This book is prompted by my daily strolls with my canine companions and, except for the nature notes and the antics of my dogs, the twenty-two gentle tales are entirely works of fiction.

Yet, despite this, there *is* an element of truth in each story. What that might be is for the reader to decide.

Brian MacDonald
January 2005

One ~ Characters And Companions

People visit Two Tree Island for any number of reasons.

I suppose my own interest in the island stems from my twice-daily walks with my dogs, and it is the dogs and their owners that I meet on which I chiefly focus. Indeed, it has been said that the dog walkers form a sort of club as we seem to meet the same people at around the same time every day and so gradually get to know each other quite well.

Nonetheless, there is always something interesting to see or hear, and I have walked the island even on the rare and temporary occasions I have not had a dog.

Companionship is the thing that strikes you about the dog-walkers. They may take a stroll round the island with another dog owner, but their true companion is almost always their dog.

Mankind has a special relationship with the dog, and for millennia has formed its own special bond with its four-footed companions. The ancient Egyptians venerated dogs and bred them for hunting, walking, guarding and, as one Egyptologist once put it, 'for the parlour.' Since you only invite your closest friends into your parlour, it is clear that even in ancient times dogs were sometimes kept just for pure companionship.

I can think of any number of acquaintances I have seen on Two Tree whose main companion in life has been their beloved dog. Old Les and Annie (see Chapter Two) are a case in point, but there are many others. The middle-aged gentlemen whose marriage was a constant trial to him was kept sane by the relationship he had with a lovely bitch retriever, the widow whose consolation was in her new spaniel puppy.

We all of us find a kind of love and affection from our devoted animals which demand very little in return; food, affectionate attention and regular walks.

I've often said that no matter how bad your day has been in the office, how dreadful the commuting was that evening or what mood you might be in when you return home, your dog is always pleased to see you and its pleasure and joy in greeting you again cannot fail to lighten your own spirits.

Indeed, even if I pop round to my local corner shop for an evening paper and am gone only a few minutes, the effusive welcome I get from Ollie, my present doggy companion, on my return to the house is as enthusiastic and hearty as the one I used to get from any of his predecessors in the days when I used to travel away from home for weeks on end.

Giving a home to a dog is one thing, but the downside is that they eventually sicken and die.

Any pet-owner will tell you that some of the worst moments in their lives are when they tearfully have to cradle their faithful friend in their arms as the vet administers the final suffering-ending injection.

It was Max who was the first to accompany me on my ramblings of Two Tree many years ago.

We saw him in a dog-breeder's establishment deep in the Essex countryside and instantly fell in love with what was all too temporarily a tiny black fur ball that responded sleepily to our cuddles and fondlings. Had we known better, we would have realised that his oversize paws gave warning of a creature that would have an appetite and a body to match and that, probably, the breeder was glad to have sold the dog on. It didn't matter to us, for it took no time at all for Max to become a full member of the family, and he was a great favourite with our two boys who regarded him as a friend and playmate and discussed all their childhood problems, frustrations and ambitions with him

A jet-black cross between a collie and a Labrador, Max was often mistaken for an Alsatian and was the living embodiment of the phrase 'to dog one's footsteps.' I could never leave a room without him following me; he would either flop down beside my new position or patiently wait outside the door of whichever room I happened to move to.

He also had that mysterious, but very real and rare, psychic connection to me and would always alert the family to my pending return home from work by sitting up and staring out of the living room window or by moving off to guard the front door. While Max was alive, there were never any surprise entrances to the house on my part; the family always knew when I was about to return home.

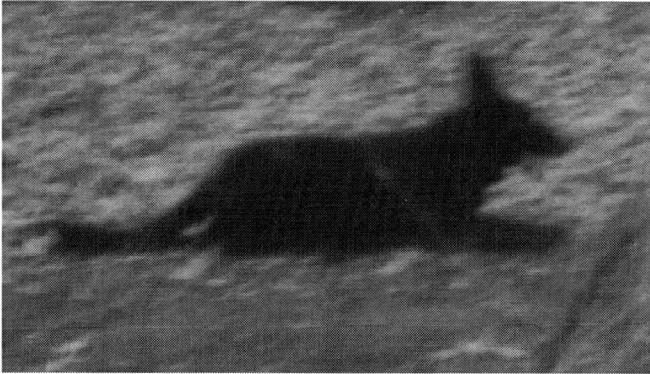

'Max'

Max was a large dog and appeared intimidating to those who didn't know him even though he was, in fact, quite amiable and gentle.

Indeed on one occasion a chum of mine, who had driven me home late one night and who rested for a while in an armchair in the living room while I went to bed, was alarmed to find when he woke that Max was sitting bolt upright on his haunches in front of him and staring menacingly, as he thought, into his eyes. As soon as the dog ambled off to another room, my chum was out of the door like a shot and afterwards took a long time to convince that he had not been in danger. Yet on the one occasion Max managed to catch a rabbit, he picked it up without harming it and carried it gently to me, laid it by my feet and then sat and took no notice whatsoever when it recovered and slowly lolloped off back off into the bushes.

As Max got older he was joined by Ben, a Lancashire Heeler, a busy, bossy, brave little fellow with short legs, a stout body and a constantly erect tail. Owned originally by a gentleman of the road who became sick and needed long-term hospitalisation, Ben was taken to an animal rescue centre where a little while later we spotted him.

We were fortunate to get him, for a young couple with two small grizzling children in front of us in the queue were also after him. However, the lady in charge said that the centre's staff were uncertain of Ben's temperament and thought he might possibly be aggressive to children. So we got him and in fact, he turned out to have a lovely temperament and was never any trouble.

Ben livened Max's life up considerably and they became inseparable, especially when out for walks. They played together and often used to grab the sticks I threw, running along the paths with the stick between their jaws looking very like diminutive horses pulling a chariot. Over time as Max slowed up, Ben would reconnoitre the ground ahead and attempt to protect Max from any suspicious oncomers.

'Ben'

Max had a long and active life, but at the age of fifteen he had reached the end of his road and a last visit to the vet's could not be avoided for his sake. The change in Ben was marked; he clearly missed his mate just as much as the rest of us did and so, a few months later, we went in search of another dog.

Spotting a sign outside a house in the street where my in-laws lived advertising Jack Russell puppies for sale, we knocked on the door and were shown into a grubby kitchen where half a dozen puppies were corralled in a large cardboard box. There we spotted the seemingly vulnerable, mewing runt of the litter that, according to our lights, definitely needed looking after. A few pounds changed hands and he was ours. Another unwanted dog admitted to the wanting Clan MacDonald.

His tail had not been docked, his legs were a bit on the short side, his ears flopped over and rarely stuck up and he looked for all the world like Piglet in the Winnie the Pooh books our boys enjoyed so much. So he was swiftly named Piglet, and in short time this name evolved into Piggy.

'Piggy'

Piggy and Ben bonded very quickly and it was interesting to see how Ben took it upon himself to train the new arrival into the ways of living with humans. Piggy never had to be house trained, as Ben did it. Piggy never had to be taught to behave himself when out for walks, as Ben did it. Ben did all his training and Piggy, by watching and learning, was soon begging for scraps, sitting when told and doing all the things we owners like our dogs to do.

Piggy often gave the impression that he was stupid. Brain-dead our boys averred, for although given basic training by Ben, he would sometimes stare intently into space as if watching an invisible person moving about the living room. This could sometimes be more than a little disconcerting and led to our wondering on occasions whether we really did have unseen visitors in the house.

Stung on the muzzle by a bee in the garden one day, he still persisted in chasing them but, thinking they were giant bees, would go into paroxysms of fear when model aircraft were flown too low or noisily when out for walks on Two Tree. I never subscribed to the theory that he was either vulnerable or brain-dead, for I was of the opinion that Piggy had carefully observed humankind and gauged correctly how best to manipulate it.

The two dogs became inseparable and, once again, we were to observe them each grabbing the end of a stick and running with it in their jaws like charioteers.

And then it was Ben's turn to disappear. He had developed diabetes and that caused additional problems, and at the age of ten we had to say good-bye to this little character. And then Piggy was on his own and his loneliness showed.

Some months later I was to be seen scouring the local animal shelters once again, but none of the very many dogs I saw sparked that special 'something' that tells you that you have found a new friend. Until the day when I spotted Soda and, not long after that she became part of the Clan MacDonald.

Part of a brother and sister pair that had to be separated and rehomed, Soda was a four-year old Jack Russell cross with long legs and a feathery, quivering, dancing question-mark of a tail. I first saw her when I did the weekly rounds of the local animal shelters, and in the third one I visited, she immediately came running up to say hello.

An hour or so later, I bought one of my sons back to the shelter to give an opinion on her and, once again, Soda came running up to greet us. A little later my wife came back with me to see her and the result was a foregone conclusion and we became her third owner.

Soda's reaction on arriving at our house was an interesting one. She stepped inside the front door and, like a tornado, immediately toured the house at top speed and then made straight for the living room and the settee where, Bambi-like, she curled herself up into a tight ball and fell asleep much to Piggy's astonishment. Soda had arrived and evidently she liked what she saw. The poor animal was a bag of bones and had a number of problems that were quickly sorted out by our vet and she soon settled into the house, despite Piggy being somewhat put out by the new arrival.

'Soda'

After a couple of weeks of growling stand-offs Piggy decided that he had neither the energy or the inclination to be the top-dog, and so he willingly conceded that position to Soda who, in any event, had already decided that she was the top-dog and didn't know what all the fuss had been about.

Soda was a loving, gentle soul who liked her creature comforts and was most definitely my wife's dog. She was a timid animal when out walking but we noticed that she had a wily side for, if she spotted dogs approaching that looked vaguely menacing, she would dance around Piggy barking loudly in an attempt to rouse him to go on the offensive. Most times Piggy just couldn't be bothered; all he ever wanted was a quiet life.

Once again two dogs became a team and could be seen snuffling around the paths together, each checking out any scent discovered by the other and keeping a close eye on each other.

And then, at the age of fifteen, it was Piggy's turn to disappear from our lives and I unashamedly confess that, many years later, I miss that little fellow more than any other dog we have had over the years. I always had a soft spot for the little half-pint; he was a great character who had very many endearing ways and, apart from being a bit stand-offish with people he didn't like, had no harm in him at all.

To our surprise Soda seemed unaffected by Piggy's passing. She was unquestionably a self-contained animal, content with her own company, though I always thought that she missed being able to boss Piggy around as she did.

So for a long time, Soda remained an only dog and she never gave any sign that she minded this. And when we took in a neighbour's dog, Judy, after her owner became ill and later died Soda never gave any recognition that the new animal existed; in her mind she carried on being an only dog.

Judy was a miniature Yorkshire terrier and a more timid, placid and quiet creature cannot be imagined. We had known her for many years as we were friends of her owner and, though she was a sweet little thing and always pleased to see us, she did not exist as far as Soda was concerned. Soda always completely ignored her presence.

The new dog had a skin condition that gave her a great deal of discomfort. But daily washes and massages with a medicated shampoo prescribed by our vet along with tablets for her other ailments followed by some professional grooming, and a month later Judy was the veritable bee's knees and looked terrific. With her skin problem treated Judy perked up no end and, doubtless prompted by my daily treatments, Judy became *my* dog. Once again, I had a friend that couldn't bear to be out of my sight and she would follow me everywhere around the house.

If in the eyes of Soda, Judy existed then she didn't show it. Except when we were out for walks and Soda decided to check a scent that Judy had herself investigated, Soda showed no sign that Judy was present. We interpreted this, probably correctly, as Soda being entirely comfortable with Judy's presence and that Judy presented no threat whatsoever to her senior position in the household.

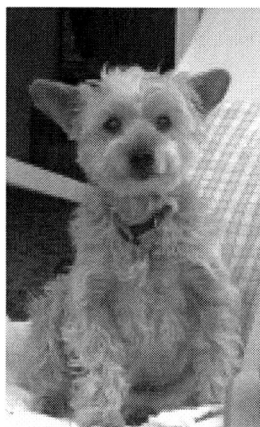

'Judy'

Alas, we had Judy for only seven months, for she developed an inoperable tumour that finally led to her having to be put to sleep to prevent any further suffering.

We missed the little creature dreadfully, for Judy was absolutely no trouble whatsoever in the short time she was with us.

And then not very long afterwards it was dear Soda's turn to make that hated last visit to the vet's, and another little animal's suffering was ended while I tearfully held her in my arms and felt the life-force ebb as she slipped away.

Soda was fifteen when we lost her and in the eleven years she was with us could not have been a better companion. She was well-mannered, gentle and absolutely no trouble at all except on the occasions she could smell a fox, at which times she would turn into a uncontrollable raging beast champing at the bit to hunt the interloper down and kill it - though she fortunately never managed to catch one.

Soda was such a character and so much in tune with our ways and routines that the house felt completely empty and soulless without her. It says much that the three other adults living in the house agreed with me on this, and eventually I couldn't stand being without a canine companion. I went in search of a new friend.

It took many months and many fruitless visits to animal rescue centres, but eventually I saw a dog that ignited that special spark in my mind. My wife checked him out, the animal rescue organisation checked us out and then he was ours.

Enter Ollie, a seven-month old undocked and long-tailed, short-legged little Jack Russell cross with one blue and one brown eye that in many ways reminds us of Piggy; indeed, there are occasions when we don't have our brains in gear and call him Piggy by mistake. It doesn't matter to him, he answers to either name.

Originally named Max - an inappropriate name for such a little half-pint fellow! - he was rehomed when his owner could no longer cope with a young puppy and a new baby. He is now nearly two years old and adapted to his new home and surroundings very quickly.

'Ollie'

Ollie will probably be our last canine friend (unless we get him a companion, which is what we are considering at the time of writing), for if he lives his natural span we feel we will be too old to start again with a replacement. Not in many years have we had a puppy in the house, but we have adapted to his exuberance and puppy ways. We are not sure that he has adapted much to our habits and routines and have the suspicion, as I had with Piggy, that it is he who is adept in the ways of manipulating humans to adapt to his requirements.

Ollie, who is incredibly friendly to people and other dogs, has one fault that we have had to deal with; he is an escape artist always ready for adventure, and we have to make sure that he is safely corralled every time the front door is open. This is not always easy with a dog that is both speedy and as slippery as an eel but, with one exception, we have coped so far.

His predilection for adventure was first discovered when the little half-pint fellow slipped out of the front door when it was opened to the postman and he was off down our road, round the corner and across a busy main road in almost as many seconds as it has taken me to write these words. I chased after him but he was already out of sight; the sounds of screeching car brakes showed me the direction he had taken and one shaken driver kindly pointed me to the side-road into which he had shot at high speed. This was, fortunately, a cul-de-sac and he was easily gathered into my trembling arms and heaving chest and bought safely back home.

We discovered also that Ollie has exceptionally good eyesight – far better than any of our previous dogs - and, given half a chance, will shoot off to say hello to any people or dogs that he can see in the far distance.

If you spot a half-pint, long-tailed Jack Russell with one blue and one brown eye, brown patches on his ears and black patches on his body and short legs on Two Tree Island, then you will know that it is Ollie. If you see the little fellow off the lead, then please hang on to him for I will be sure to be soon pounding up the path breathlessly behind him.

This story is probably no different from that of any other pet owner, for most of us absorb our pets completely into our lives, invest them with human-like qualities and treat them as part of the family.

This is demonstrated to me every day down on Two Tree Island in the way I see the walkers reacting to their dogs and, much more sadly, to their deaths. There are a number of dogs which have been buried on Two Tree and a couple of their graves were marked with stones. Memories of happier days were kept alive by the occasional visit and sometimes by the placing of flowers on the graves.

I used to see a lovely couple walk the island with a beautifully groomed and gentle greyhound, Alice, and when it died it was buried in an out of the way part of the park and every day the grave, which was marked with white pebbles, was kept tended by the old couple.

And then the husband, Harry, died and I would only see his widow who continued to come down to the island on her own each day for a walk and to keep Alice's grave neat and tidy. Sometimes, she would put a small posy of flowers in a jar on the stone-outlined grave. I asked her one morning why she kept up this duty every day in all weathers and was surprised by her response.

'Why, Harry's ashes are right there alongside Alice's!'

You have to admit that there are worse places to spend eternity than on Two Tree Island and alongside your faithful canine friend and companion.

I never did find out whether Harry's widow eventually joined them as well, though I would like to think so.

Heaven
(A DIY Haiku)

There is no heaven
If absent from that heaven
Are our canine* friends.

* *Insert here as required, feline, equine, porcine, bovine, furry, human - or whatever!*

Two ~ Les and Annie

Distinguished at all times of the year by a heavy tweed jacket fastened with a bit of twine, patched grey trousers and with a dewdrop trembling at the end of his hooked-nose, Les Forrest was in his mid-eighties.

Though now bent and stiff he still managed a turn round Two Tree Island most mornings when he reckoned, 'T'was good to get some fresh air,' even on those winter days when biting winds roaring up from the estuary made me pull the collars of my coat tighter together. Accompanied by a placid cross-terrier, Annie, who was herself of extreme age and never known to bark or make any other noise whatsoever, Les was always grateful for a bit of company and from time to time we would stroll the paths with our dogs exploring the path ahead together.

Les was an Essex man born and bred, and at some time in his youth had been a farm worker from which days grew his love of open spaces and the fresh air. A short spell as a fisherman on the cockle boats that ply from Old Leigh gave him also a taste for the sea, and his morning walks reminded him of both, especially in the early spring when the soft breezes bought with them the mixed scents of wild flowers and rotting cockleshells.

Shortly after he married, his wife apparently persuaded him to take a job ashore and, until he retired, Les stoically plodded away in a local factory assembling parts for electrical equipment. It was mind-numbing work but, as he told me many times, it let his mind wander the summer fields and the mirror-calm seas of the Essex coast in perfect freedom. 'There's a lot to be said for they factories,' he once said, 'When yer mind's wandering in the past, the sun's always high in the sky and there's never any bad weather.'

Prodded by his wife, about whom he rarely spoke, Les bought a small semi-detached bungalow in Leigh and had lived there ever since. For the last twenty-odd years since his wife died he had lived there with only a dog, always a terrier, for company.

Annie was the only companion Les needed and he talked to her as if she were human, asking her what she thought of the morning's weather, whether she thought it might rain later on and if she fancied a bit of fish for her dinner and so on. ''Ain't got no family,' he once said, 'The dog's all the family I need.'

Whether, or quite how, the two communicated I do not know, but Les swore that they did and that he always knew what the dog was thinking. Some days Annie fancied fish and other days she fancied meat, and Les was happy to oblige since he ate the same food that he prepared for the dog, including those occasions when he made a Shepherd's Pie as a treat, ''Cos we all needs a treat now an' agin.'

He and Annie would walk down the hill each morning from Leigh and in the long light summer days could be seen on Two Tree from around six o'clock and from daybreak in the winter.

Despite having no family, Les was perfectly happy with his lot in life though he strongly thought the government ('Miserable tight-fisted bureaucratic buggers!') should improve the old-age pension. He loved his garden and would sometimes share his runner beans, peas and tomatoes with those of us that strolled with him in the mornings.

During the day Les shared working his garden with watching the television soaps and the news bulletins, but three evenings a week were spent in one of the pubs in Old Leigh where he would sip two half-pints of beer, play a few rounds of dominoes and walk down Memory Lane with a rapidly diminishing group of old cronies and with Annie sitting by his side.

Les was old in body, but it should not be thought that he was old in spirit. On the contrary, his mind was as sharp as ever and he kept up to date with world affairs through his television set and would often surprise you with a succinct judgement of the latest political issue backed up by a brief summary of the pros and cons of whatever situation interested him.

I have seen him take on younger men, self-superior in their education and supposed knowledge of world affairs, and reduce them to silence after a few minutes during which he would give an accurate and interesting analysis of the latest issue of the day. During his morning walks, he preferred the company of those who were prepared to have what he called a 'proper natter' and not just indulge in polite, but what he thought was idle, chit-chat. Consequently, those of us that walked with him from time to time were often rewarded by the discussions we had.

In health, Les had been extremely lucky, though he was rather proud of the fact that he had his appendix removed when in his early seventies. He needed no regular medication and was happy to tell anyone foolish enough to mention their own ailments that regular meals, an occasional pint of ale and a bit of exercise with a good dog every day was all that most men needed to ensure a long and healthy life.

But, as the years wore on, it became increasingly obvious that Les was slowing up, winter colds sometimes turned to bronchitis and there were spells when he went missing for a week or two at a stretch. Always he would bounce back and be seen with Annie slowly strolling the paths of Two Tree and nattering to those patient enough to match his pace and wait while he waited for Annie to finish sniffing at some interesting spot that held an animal scent.

It was early in June that Les and Annie last went missing, and for weeks us regulars of Two Tree wondered whether anything had happened to either of them. Surely, if Annie had died Les would not now bother to replace her. On the other hand, perhaps something had happened to Les himself, but as none of us knew quite where he lived we could not check.

In the event, it did not matter for I came upon them one beautiful summer morning five weeks later when out walking with Ben.

He was about halfway round the usual circuit and both he and Annie seemed to me to be somewhat sprightlier than usual. He did not mention the reason for his absence but, as we strolled together, it was clear that he was in excellent form and we talked about the summer flowers, the ripening blackberries, the skylarks chattering high in the sky and the sight of the mud flats being worked over by squawking gulls and other birds. 'This is my favourite spot,' Les said, 'And I'd rather be here than anywhere else.'

I knew what he meant for, indeed, it was a glorious morning and a cool breeze gently bent the grasses and bought us the faint sounds of ship's engines far out in the estuary and the scent of freshly cut grass.

We chatted about a mutual love of open spaces and the sea and our ability to enjoy both on Two Tree Island, and Les said it was a great shame that those who lived in cities and who rarely walked more than one hundred yards without looking for transport of some kind could not see this little part of the Essex coast and enjoy its peace and tranquillity.

Before going down to Two Tree next day I called into the baker's shop in Leigh for some fresh rolls and happened upon George Mitchell, who I sometimes meet with his Great Dane in the mornings and who was also a chum of Les.

'Did you hear about poor old Les?' he asked. 'Annie died about a month ago and Les buried her on Two Tree. He died two days later. Broken-hearted, I would guess.'

I was shocked but, in a way, I was not surprised, for Les was now free to walk his favourite bit of the coast in perfect freedom with his beloved dog, Annie.

It is said that ghosts are most usually seen when it is cold and dark and on those occasions when one's senses are more attuned to one's surroundings. There is undoubtedly more indirect and ambient light generally than, say, one hundred or more years ago and this may, according to some theories, be the reason why the number of ghostly sightings have reduced over that time. And, perhaps, the increasing light levels over recent years have resulted in a dimming of some of our own senses.

Against this, it was broad daylight when I met Les and, in any event, I don't know of a single instance where anyone has had a conversation with a ghost. Nor do I understand why I should have been selected for a natter with Les for, so far as I know, no-one else has since.

Others who are knowledgeable about supernatural matters assert that the stonework of ancient buildings, old castles and churches for example, somehow absorb emotionally charged moments in time and are able to play them back when the conditions are right or when the ground has been disturbed. But, here again, these factors were not at play when I met Les.

Just a little while ago, a visiting neighbour mentioned that her dog often went into the hall and stared at a particular spot, and she wondered if the house had its own resident ghost. My wife was quite shocked at hearing this, for she happened to be present when the previous owner had collapsed and died on that self same spot.

At the time, I was reminded of Piggy who used to stop and look at a spot in our living room (though none of our other dogs ever have since) and I was reminded also of dear old Les and Annie.

On the rare occasion I still see Les and Annie on my morning walks, though curiously enough never in the afternoons. Both Les and Annie look as solid and alive as you or I as we walk Two Tree Island, but I have never since been able to get close enough to chat again with him.

If you see them, you'll recognise Les. His usual battered tweed jacket fastened with a bit of twine and patched grey trousers, slightly bent and often talking to a small cross-terrier that never makes a noise.

Oh, and a dewdrop trembling on the end of his hooked-nose whatever the time of year.

Three ~ I Heard One Day

I am often up and about by five o'clock in the morning, sometimes earlier in summer, a throwback to when I married and had to get up at an early hour as part of a job I had at that time. The principles of Pavlov's dog kicked in from the second day at work and I have never been able to get myself out of the habit of waking early, even at weekends and when on holiday.

Oftentimes rising early is a curse, especially to my sleeping partner, but getting up early often has its rewards, and this is particularly so on those occasions when I take an early morning stroll round Two Tree Island on high-summer days when the air is cool and still and I can enjoy the sights and sounds of the island as well as its tranquility.

What one notices is how the bird song and other noises form their own, mainly fixed, pockets of overlapping territorial sound which one moves into and out of as one strolls around.

The resident pheasant seems in the main to inhabit only one small area of the reserve, the ducks and other wild fowl tend to stick around the ponds, the reservoir and the salt marsh, and the skylarks usually stay in the same area around the park. There are areas in which the rabbits predominate and other areas where they are absent; the former can often be sensed by the earthy smell they leave around since they rarely make a noise other than the occasionally heard stamping of a warning foot.

Not all the birds are territorial.

The cuckoos fly around everywhere in search of a mate or an attractive nest. The gulls, crows and magpies, equally as raucous and noisy as the other, also appear to regularly quarter the island in search of food and the curious, playful swallows will very often circle around you as you walk the paths. The hawks and other raptors can be seen just about everywhere as their sharp eyes search for food.

The bird song is extremely varied and an absolute delight to listen to as one takes a walk but, in my humble view at any rate, that of the blackbird is the most tuneful to listen to.

There are a number of blackbirds resident on Two Tree and their song lifts the soul in the early mornings as the island comes alive and the birds call to each other or remind their neighbours of the extent of their territories.

There are other sounds, of course.

The hum of a ship's engine out in the estuary or the puttering sound of a cockleboat's engine, the rattling of a train as it goes through the points at Leigh Station, the siren of an emergency vehicle rushing along the London Road above the Downs or the roar of an aircraft taking off from Southend Airport. Alas, there are also sometimes the noisy bass sounds vibrating out of the stereo systems of cars of the youngsters who come down to the island to carouse with their friends; fortunately these are but rarely heard in the mornings.

People occasionally form pockets of noise of their own as they move around Two Tree.

The happy sounds of a chattering couple of ladies I used to call Gert and Daisy (see Chapter Ten), for example, fade into the distance as they move away from the car park and reappear thirty minutes or so later as they swing back round towards it. The chap that trains his non-existent gun-dog is another case in point; as he moves around, his dog-whistle fades and then returns from time to time as he quarters the reserve quite oblivious to the astonished stares that he generates.

And then there used to be the sound of Wallace Morgan, a Welshman with a rich, deep bass baritone voice and who used his morning walks on Two Tree to practice for the next performance of one of the local operatic societies.

Wallace was an extremely shy man and it was amazing to me that he was ever able to get up on a stage and sing so beautifully but, as he told me one day, his intense nervousness left him the very instant he stepped on stage. He found the best place to rehearse his music was when walking his dachshund on Two Tree early in the mornings, though he always stopped singing if saw people coming into view.

Thus it was that one would sometimes hear snatches of the most lovely music emanating from Wallace's direction some mornings; the stirring 'Tuba Mirum' from Mozart's Requiem or the delicate 'Omnia Sol Temperat' from Carl Orff's Carmina Burana, for example.

A walk on Two Tree, at least while Wallace still lived in the area, could be most entertaining sometimes.

But Wallace's favourite music was much less highbrow than the pieces I have just mentioned, beautiful though they are, for he was an aficionado of the Gilbert & Sullivan operettas and of The Mikado in particular.

I can recall many mornings when I heard snatches of various songs from The Mikado and, as someone also fond of Gilbert & Sullivan's music, it was inevitable that as I walked I might hum the tune I heard or, on the occasion that I knew the words, sing along with Wallace, but well away from him and in a much softer voice.

'As Someday It Must Happen That a Victim Must be Found,' 'I Am So Proud,' 'A More Humane Mikado' and so on were songs of his that I could sometimes sing along to, taking care not to be overheard by anyone else who might be around.

There were occasions when Wallace was obviously rehearsing a particular piece, and repetitive snatches of these would be the only ones you would hear coming from his direction.

There were other instances when Wallace was just enjoying himself and singing all manner of excerpts from the Gilbert & Sullivan operettas, including those for soprano and contralto. Songs such as 'I am a Maiden,' for instance, could be a little confusing for anyone who actually knew the songs that were being delivered in a wonderful bass baritone.

Now and again Wallace and I might walk together and chat about choral music and about the Gilbert & Sullivan operettas and their clever patter songs. He was very unimpressed when I told him that I had performed on the stage of Covent Garden a couple of times, but highly amused when I admitted that I was dressed as a goblin and my 'performance' only amounted to rushing across the stage along with some of my schoolmates screaming in Wagner's Das Rheingold.

At the end of a particularly hot summer when the local water authority had once again declared a drought in the area, and shortly before Wallace retired and returned to his Welsh birthplace, the most delightful thing occurred that, to the other person involved, we still remember with not a little pride.

It happened that Wallace was rehearsing for The Mikado and was singing his part from a trio; Ko-Ko, Pooh-Bah and Pish-Tush, who sing their separate parts to begin with and then blend their words into an harmonious whole.

I was walking across the rough track between the two main paths of the park one morning with Max who, as usual, was snuffling along with his head down among the tall grasses and following the scent of some small animal. Strolling slowly along the metalled path by the Sea Scout Hut was Wallace who could be heard singing the part of Ko-Ko.

'My brain it teems
With endless schemes
Both good and new
For Titipu ...'

When another chap approached from the opposite direction and started to sing the part of Pish-Tush.

'I heard one day
A gentleman say
That criminals who
Are cut in two
Can hardly feel
The fatal steel ...'

The two men quickly synchronised their efforts and the effect

24

was brilliant on a sunny morning with no breeze and no other sounds except the skylarks singing high in the sky.

A more perfect setting for men to be singing could hardly be imagined.

How could I resist? I couldn't. So I crossed over to the main path and, linking up with the other two, and with Max wondering what on earth I was up to, joined in with the Pooh-Bah part.

'I am so proud
If I allowed
My family pride
To be my guide,
I'd volunteer ...'

Perhaps if the music of Gilbert and Sullivan does not appeal to the reader or if the reader himself does not sing, this tale may not mean a great deal.

All I can say is that to three men that particular morning, Gilbert & Sullivan came alive in a very special way and our three voices blended beautifully - well, I thought so! - just for a few minutes; Wallace the seasoned performer and two men who would be scared witless if asked to sing in public.

Three voices, singing their separate parts but coming together in a perfect harmony:

'To sit in solemn silence in a dull, dark dock,
In a pestilential prison, with a lifelong lock,
Awaiting the sensation of a short, sharp shock,
From a cheap and chippy chopper on a big black block!'

Bird song you can hear every day on Two Tree Island - but not necessarily Gilbert & Sullivan!

Four ~ Of Ships ... and Things

My working life was spent in the shipping industry and it is my good fortune that Two Tree Island is sometimes a good place from which to see the shipping in the Thames Estuary.

Countless times have I settled for a little while with my dog and watched the cruise ships steam up towards London or head back down and out to sea. We have seen the replicas of Peter the Great's *Shtandart* and Captain Cook's *Endeavour* pass by in full sail on their maiden voyages up to London and also watched the largest sailing ship in the world, *Star Clipper*, gracefully pass one evening with all of its sails unfurled and doing quite a speed as it headed down towards Southend Pier on its maiden cruise.

Many people come down to the island to watch the ships and most of them head for the Coast Guard cabin down by the boat hard and the launching ramp where, once the ships pass by Canvey Island, there are unobstructed views of the estuary at sea level. Armed with the local newspaper or one of the shipping magazines which publish the timetables of passenger and other interesting ships, you may now and again spot a ship enthusiast on the hard equipped with binoculars and camera.

There are those whose interests are primarily in passenger ships, but there are also those who don't mind what the ship is and who are just as pleased to see a car-carrier, container ship, dredger, tanker or even a warship sail by. Like train spotters, they make a note of the ship's name and check to see whether there has been any recent change in the ship's livery or modification to the superstructure.

Many of these people are extraordinarily knowledgeable about ships and their various characteristics and routes, and when prompted will reel off all sorts of interesting facts, the previous names of this ship or the different uses to which that ship has been put over the years. Many times has my knowledge of the vessels of my own company been put to shame by one of the expert shipping enthusiasts I see occasionally on Two Tree.

Roger Mason was one of these and I had known him for many years as he worked in the London office of my own company.

Roger had been an accounts clerk all of his working life and he readily admitted that it was the most utterly boring occupation that anyone could possibly wish to find. That was the downside. But, and in Roger's mind it was a big but, the upside was that it was a strictly nine to five job which carried no responsibility or worries whatsoever. He got paid a decent wage at the end of every month and that wage enabled Roger and his wife to do all sorts of interesting things. It would be overstating it to say that Roger was a Jekyll and Hyde character, but there were unquestionably two sides to his life. He was the unobtrusive clerk during the day, working exactly from nine to five with a sixty-minute lunch break, but at night and at weekends he was a changed man completely.

Where he found the time to do all the things he did was beyond me, especially as I was usually exhausted at the end of a long working day plus the dreadful commute to London (Oh God, that awful commute to and from London!), but Roger found time to take an Open University degree, run a smallholding producing eggs and vegetables, be a member of an amateur dramatic society, the chairman of a photographic club *and* play an active role in the running of his local church.

In addition to all these activities, plus doing his day job, Roger was an authority on the history of British shipping and his annual holidays, usually taken in four one-week bites, took him and his wife to the major ports in the world where he managed to combine his shipping interests with that of photography.

When Roger retired some years ago, he was fortunate enough to be selected as a lecturer by two of the cruise lines and you can well imagine that he was in his seventh heaven. Latterly though, his wife's health had not been too good and Roger had given up his lecturing and their holidays were now mainly taken in Britain where he reckoned his wife had access to a decent health service whenever it was needed.

Nonetheless, I would still see Roger down on Two Tree now and again and on these occasions I would not fail to wander over to where he was standing and have a natter.

Late one damp and chilly afternoon just before Fireworks Night and with Max trotting along beside me, I came across Roger sitting on a folding stool in the car park near the Coast Guard cabin and looking through his binoculars over the estuary where there was not a ship in sight save for a car-carrier heading out to sea in the far distance. I was curious to know what he was looking for because the silhouette of Canvey Island blocks out most of the ships' profiles except for their superstructures and I could not see anything moving on the river behind it.

Roger was so engrossed in looking through his binoculars that he did not hear my approach or respond to Max giving his knee the nudge that would usually trigger a bit of fussing. Whatever was to be seen out on the water was occupying Roger's mind completely.

I asked him what he was looking for so intently and was surprised to be told that he really didn't know. You can't let a comment like that escape and I persisted.
  'Look through the glasses across the estuary towards the power station,' he said, handing me the binoculars. 'See if you can see anything in midstream in front of it.'
  I looked carefully in the direction he gave me. The power station on the Kent coast could be seen very clearly but there was absolutely nothing to be seen on the placid water between it and where we were standing.
  'What are you looking for? I asked.
  'I just don't know!' came the exasperated answer once again.

Roger is one of the most sensible people I know and something was obviously troubling him. Shortly he put his glasses away and told me what it was.

He explained that the evening before, he had gone down to Two Tree with his camera equipment, which he had set up in the same car park. He went there to photograph a new container ship sailing out to sea with all of its lights ablaze as this would make a good picture. A slow-moving haze of light above and behind Canvey Island to the right showed him that he was in good time and he was waiting patiently for the ship to emerge from behind the island and move in front of him.

The camera equipment was all set up in readiness and Roger poured himself a cup of coffee from a flask he had bought down. He had plenty of time before the ship appeared and he was looking up and down the estuary to see if there were any other ships moving.

He didn't spot a ship, but what he did see caused him to drop his coffee mug in surprise.

Coming up river from the direction of Southend Pier and appearing to be at some considerable height and close to the Kent coast was a very bright ball of yellow light that moved so fast it left a contrail of light behind it which was clearly reflected in the waters of the Estuary. At a point seemingly just in front of the power station, the light did a sharp ninety-degree turn towards the water and abruptly disappeared around one hundred feet or so above the surface of the river.

The whole experience lasted just three or four seconds and left Roger completely baffled as to what he had just seen.

It could have been a firework, I ventured to suggest, but Roger didn't think this was the explanation. 'Even fireworks can't travel four or five miles at such a speed and they don't make sudden ninety degree turns. Besides which, the light was a consistent bright yellow which never changed in hue or shape and it didn't give off any sparks.'

It was a mystery one had to admit and one that we have discussed many times since. Roger repeatedly came back to the island both at night and in daylight over the next few days but could find no clue whatsoever to what he had seen.

He is certain that the light did not enter the water and, having seen many fireworks being let off over the following few days, is quite convinced that what he saw was neither a firework nor one of the old ship's flares which are sometimes let off at this time of year in these parts.

I tend to agree with Roger that what he saw that night might have been some kind of UFO, though quite what it was or what it was doing could not be guessed.

A few weeks later, my wife saw in one of the local newspapers a story which said that the town of Basildon, a few miles inland in the direction of London, was the Essex UFO window. Not having seen a UFO myself, I cannot express an opinion, but it does lend a sort of credence to what Roger thought he saw that night from Two Tree Island.

The pity of it all was that Roger was so anxious to discover the cause of the strange light, that he quite failed to photograph the brand-new container ship that shortly afterwards passed in full front of him with all of its lights blazing.

Five ~ Dorothea's Mount

Over the years I have been fortunate to live temporarily in various places including Australia, California, Alaska and Spain. In none of these places did the weather prove particularly troublesome for me, though I frequently got drenched in Monsoon rains when visiting India.

But, of course, you don't have to go as far as India to be caught in Monsoon-type downpours.

It was winter, the rain was bucketing down and Max and I were completely soaked to the skin as we took a somewhat sodden walk round Two Tree Island's park.

My anorak that morning was completely useless and Max's tail, usually held jauntily erect like a furry ship's pennant, was dripping wet and stowed beneath his rump. Now and again he stopped to shake off the surplus water which his so-called waterproof coat had started to soak up.

It was certainly wet, as evidenced by the many puddles and the drooping, dripping trees and plants. The Thames Estuary was hidden behind a wall of rain and, so heavy was the downpour, I could only just make out the edge of Benfleet Creek.

But as I frequently tell people, there is always something to see on Two Tree Island and this morning was no exception despite the pouring rain.

What caught my eye this day were the number of snails that had climbed the skeletal remains of the ground-elder and hedge-parsley not far from the park entrance. Over a fairly small area, there were many hundreds of snails of all sizes making their way slowly up the bare stems of the plants or perched precariously on their bony waving tips.

The snails that had arrived at the top of these dead plants did not seem to be doing anything except for just clinging on for dear life in the wind and rain, and I wondered what the purpose of this marathon trek and climb was all about.

It was a very odd sight, and one that I have not seen since and one which no-one has been able to explain to me. Even more curious was the fact that the climbing snails were to be seen only in this particular patch of ground and nowhere else along the path that Max and I took that morning.

While I was bent over one plant looking closely at the colourful whorls on the shell of one small snail, Dorothea Wilson came up behind me with her little Corgi, Joffry, and asked me what I was paying such close attention to in such dreadful weather.

I had known Dorothea for around two years and she was one of the most interesting women that I ever met. One never really knows the people one meets when one is out and about but, in Dorothea's case, I did get to know her during our brief meetings on Two Tree Island and on the occasions she came over to our house for supper.

Dorothea was in her 80's and becoming somewhat frail. Nonetheless, she walked a bit of the park now and again with Joffry and was a delight to talk to.

Dorothea was the only child of an Assize Court Judge who married into money, and in due course she inherited the lot. The money permitted Dorothea to live life in some considerable comfort and she made full use of it, travelling extensively and becoming patron of a number of local charitable societies.

Dorothea, a very down to earth old lady, lived in a smart Georgian house close to the sea front and, until she felt she got too old for it, delighted in giving dinner parties to her vast network of chums and acquaintances, and sometimes letting the local children's society have use of her large garden in the summer to raise funds with a fete.

Driving a splendid old red Jaguar, in the back seat of which Joffry rode in style on a tartan blanket, one would sometimes see Dorothea out shopping in Leigh. She would occasionally be found also in a small French restaurant in Southend of which she was very fond and whose owner allowed Joffry to sit quietly under the table by her chair.

In her younger days Dorothea had enjoyed walking and climbing and was only too pleased to tell how she had once climbed the Matterhorn, the lower slopes of Everest as well as many other peaks, and of the various expeditions she had undertaken in the places that other people dream about or see on television documentaries.

Just a couple of years ago, she had done a tour by boat of the little villages lining Russia's White Sea. With seven companions, she had coped with coffin-sized sleeping berths, little or no deck or living space, poor food and tin cans for wash basin and loo. Despite the discomfort and lack of facilities, she had a whale of a time and was planning a repeat visit.

These days she supported her weary legs with an Alpine walking stick around which were fixed the many commemorative plaques of the various places she had visited.

I enjoyed Dorothea's company and her mountaineering tales, for I have had the privilege of living, albeit briefly, in true mountain country. My first spell, alas for just a few months, was when I lived in a log cabin in the San Gabriel Mountains, north east of Los Angeles. Here, one winter, I was able to enjoy every day the invigorating air of the snow-covered mountains as well as delighting in the heat of the high desert which was just a thirty minute drive down the mountain road from where I lived. Not long afterwards I spent a year in Alaska and loved the opportunities to walk in quiet solitude in the clean fresh air and revelled at being able to be so close to nature. I walked, explored, fished, observed the plant and wild life, inspected animal tracks, panned for gold and thoroughly enjoyed every living, breathing minute of it. So there was an immediate empathy when I first met Dorothea and we found much of mutual interest to talk about.

On this particular morning Dorothea was just as interested in the mystery of the climbing snails as I was, and we fruitlessly tried to figure out what their purpose was and why they were not to be seen further along the main path where the same skeletal branches were bending in the wind and the rain.

The snails were inevitably the precursor to Dorothea telling me about some of the creepie-crawlies that she had encountered over the years, and it turned out that she didn't mind the spiders and bugs but could not abide being close to any of the giant millipedes that are to be seen in the tropics; these she thought were the most terrifying creatures imaginable.

We chatted about the Monsoon rains and walked a little way up the central path to where Max and I would turn left to go across what I called The Mount many years ago when Two Tree was first opened up to the public.

I should explain that the Mount is merely a hillock of earth twenty feet or so above the level of the main path and which gives a slightly better view of the estuary. In wet weather, the path across it is extremely slippery and the descent on the other side can be dangerous except to the sure-footed.

Dorothea had walked as far as she wanted to go and waited for Joffry to join her before returning to her car and thence to the dry and warmth of home. We chatted briefly and I happened to mention that I had named this bit of the park The Mount.

'I've walked or climbed most of the world's peaks, but not this one.' she said with a laugh.

I told Dorothea that the path was slippery and I did not think she would be up to it, particularly in this sort of weather.

'Nonsense!' she said, 'I'm not ready for my box yet!'

There and then, this indomitable woman decided that she would walk across The Mount at nine o'clock the next morning, and I agreed to accompany her.

The next morning found Max and I waiting in the car park for Dorothea. The weather was atrocious, far worse than it had been the day before, and the meaning of the expression that it was raining stair-rods was very self-evident.

Two Tree had been turned into a quagmire. The main paths had been turned into streams, and rivulets were streaming down to them from the higher ground. Overnight, yet more ponds and swamps had appeared all over the place.

Soon Dorothea's car swung into the car park and out stepped the lady herself; she seemed as if she had come kitted out for a walk in the Himalayas. Indeed the antique clothes she wore were last used in an expedition of many years before; thick sweater, corduroy walking trousers strapped to the calves, stout walking boots, an oiled cape and a lovely Swiss hat with a feather in it that quickly slumped as it got soaked. Her Alpine walking stick completed the ensemble and Joffry also came equipped for his walk with an oiled Burberry coat.

'Come on then, let's do it!' she said.

Off we went up the main path in the direction of the Tree Trunk Graveyard, noting along the way that the snails seen the previous day had all disappeared, Dorothea walking slowly with the aid of her stick and the two dogs snuffling around ahead of us with Joffry trying to keep up with an impatient Max.

We eventually got to the junction where a track would take us round the side of the model airplane field towards The Mount and we left the path and walked across the wet grass to where the ground started to climb.

There is no cover from the elements on Two Tree at any time of the year and the driving rain had soaked me by this time. Dorothea, on the other hand, was quite dry under her hat and cape. 'You have to have the correct kit in weather like this,' she said in an experienced tone.

Taking one of her arms in mine, we started the short climb and accomplished this without any great effort despite the slippery surface.

Dorothea stopped to look at the view but, of course, there was none. All that was to be seen was the driving rain which obscured all except that which lay within twenty feet or so of us.

Now Dorothea saw that the track descended at a sharper slope than before and, moreover, that it sloped away to the right.

'I can see what you mean about it being slippery and dangerous in this sort of weather,' she told me, 'but don't worry, you hang on to me!'

She meant it, of course.

Off we tottered, my arm now in Dorothea's. 'Step by step,' she counselled, placing her walking stick firmly into the ground slightly in front of her and then gradually putting her weight onto it before stepping forward.

Thirty years my senior, Dorothea showed that she knew exactly what she was doing as, one step at a time, we slowly descended The Mount; me slipping and sliding on the wet mud and grass in entirely the wrong shoes but she moving slowly and purposefully forward and trying to stabilise my jerky movements.

Dorothea counted the short steps made by her right foot, there were thirty-three in all before we reached the level ground and each of these was accomplished by her in the most deliberate and calculating manner.

'Well, we made it!' she announced with some satisfaction when we got to the bottom and from there regained the metalled path.

We had indeed and I admit to being slightly wobbly when we got to the bottom though, as I told my cynical wife afterwards, I was more anxious to prevent Dorothea from slipping and injuring her frail self. Dorothea on the other hand seemed quite unfazed by her exertions; on the contrary she expressed herself delighted at having climbed one last peak and one that had been named, albeit unofficially, by someone she knew.

'I might not climb another peak again,' she said, 'But I've climbed a little one today.'

And so she had, and we celebrated with a cup of steaming hot coffee enlivened by a shot of something sensible back at my house a little later.

Dorothea has long since passed over, and as she had no surviving relatives her estate reverted to the Crown.

Dealers emptied her house and from time to time I look round the local antique and curiosity shops to see if her Alpine walking stick is there.

You will recognise it easily for it is covered with tiny plaques from the many places Dorothea visited, but it also has the words 'Dorothea's Mount' inscribed on it.

I know that to be the case, for when we got home I carved into it the new name of the latest peak that Dorothea had climbed with my own penknife.

And utterly delighted she was with it too.

Six ~ Treasure Trove

Now and again I see people with metal detectors searching the nearby beaches at low tide and am always curious to know what they find when I see them bending over with a trowel to dig up a small object that has created a certain buzz in their earphones. One of my chums who is involved in metal-detecting tells me that they are looking for small coins and items of jewellery dropped by the folk who come to Leigh and Chalkwell to relax on the sand.

On one occasion, I saw a man with a metal detector on Two Tree Island, though I cannot imagine what he thought he might find there except for bits of old engines or rusting angle-brackets and the like.

He was quartering a patch of ground in the centre of the park beyond the Tree Trunk Graveyard well away from any path and seemingly making a very thorough job of it, turning at the end of an invisible row and moving back and forth on parallel lines. Now and again he stopped to probe the ground with a garden trowel before continuing on. Max and Ben, always curious about new sights, wandered over to the man to see what he was doing but he ignored them and, if he gave them any clue as to what he was up to, they were unable to pass the news on to me.

I have no idea whether this man had permission to use his detector on Two Tree or if he found anything of any use or value, but it struck me that, since the island was essentially a former rubbish tip, he was not likely to find anything of any great value except perhaps for scrap metal. And then it occurred to me that one man's rubbish is another man's treasure.

Like any other rubbish tip or land fill site, Two Tree may eventually become the archaeologist's dream come true, while being at the same time their worst nightmare. A dream because of the quantity and variety of stuff buried on the island, and a nightmare because it is all placed out of its original context.

Come the dawning of the new day when this present age has been all but obliterated after a nuclear catastrophe, will archaeologists be able to make sense of a site that contains the buried remains of all sorts of demolished buildings, bits of old cars and machinery and the discarded rubbish and equipment from the homes of people quite unconnected with those buildings and objects?

I doubt it. But I sometimes wonder what the archaeologists of the future will make of Two Tree and what treasures and horrors they may find in the centuries to come. The only thing that is absolutely certain is that I will not be around to discover the answer to my own question.

Not that far away from Two Tree are the remains of a spoil heap from a Victorian glass and ceramics factory. I will not say where it is, lest hordes of folk descend on it and turn the place upside down in their search for trinkets.

In fact, the site was well picked over by local folk many years ago when it was first discovered. Indeed, I confess that I took my two boys down there on a number of occasions when we sorted through the soil and debris and returned home triumphant with old beer bottles, bits of finely decorated porcelain and even a couple of small glass scent bottles. Those so-called treasures have long since been reconsidered and consigned to our own rubbish bin, and may even now be among the many tons of household debris buried on Two Tree; maybe to add yet more confusion to the archaeologists of the future.

Eventually, the number of people trespassing on someone else's land and damaging it caused the owner to level the spoil heap to the ground, and in recent years it has been extremely rare to see anyone down there. Thirty years later, I recognise that we were wrong to enter someone's land without permission and dig it over for artefacts from a bygone age and that these things are best left to the professional archaeologists.

Against this, it is also true that recent changes in the law concerning treasure trove and the rewards for finding it, together with the proliferation of television programmes on the subject of antiques and the valuable objects likely to be found in junk shops, boot sales and at auctions has stimulated an interest in the search for the item that will bring its finder a quick cash reward.

The evidence of this can be seen almost every week. The people with metal detectors to be seen on the beaches, in the fields in winter, along the ridge of Hadleigh Downs and even, on one occasion I witnessed for myself, in the grounds of Hadleigh Castle.

The lure of buried treasure is a powerful one and, as I know from my own searches of the Victorian spoil heap, highly infectious.

Then there is the proliferation of other television programmes which can result in much harm. I have in mind the many gardening programmes one sees these days which have encouraged the importation of plants and creatures which are foreign to our country and environment and also to many of our beaches being stripped of their beach-protecting pebbles.

Enter at this point in my tale Bert Duffield.

A retired bank manager, Bert was the proud owner of a dory which during the summer months he moored in Benfleet Creek, hauling it out of the water in the autumn so that he could scrape and paint its bottom and do the repairs that boat owners have to carry out each year. During these sessions, Bert would be accompanied by his old border collie, Otis, who was quite content to sit on the hard, expend as little energy as possible and just watch the world go by.

Bert's mission in life was to get the maximum possible enjoyment from his boat and when he was not out in it fishing the estuary with a chum or two, he and his wife would take a couple of friends on short trips to and from Southend Pier with the boat well stocked with food and wine. Sometimes Bert would beach the boat on the Ray, a large sand bank in the estuary near Southend which is exposed at low tide, where he and his passengers would disembark for a swim and a short and mildly alcoholic picnic before the tide turned.

Bert was well known locally and I first met him one spring when he was hard at work scraping his boat's bottom and getting it ready for the new season. I was to see him many times afterwards either in one of the pubs in Old Leigh or working on his boat.

Those of you who are familiar with our little part of Essex will know that when the tide goes out, it *really* goes out and vast areas of mud flats are exposed as the sea withdraws. Usually at low tide the only people to be seen on the flats are the bait diggers, but in summertime they are a magnet for people out to enjoy themselves and many of them head for the Ray and a swim in the estuary, for some fishing or for a picnic on the sand. Some of these folk unfortunately get trapped when they do not gauge the tides correctly and the long-suffering lifeboatmen get called out to get them out of trouble; however, that is bye the bye.

Such short escapes, if done safely, can be very relaxing and many years ago my next door neighbour and I often walked the flats over to the Ray for an evening swim when the tides were right. There was one memorable occasion when we walked back as darkness fell and were enchanted by the bright luminescence left by our foot prints in the mud, and the path we took remained lit for nearly half an hour afterwards.

One spring, I spotted Bert when out for a walk one morning on Two Tree with Max and Ben. It was a day when the warm sunshine gave promise of the summer months to come, the skylarks were calling high in the sky and, with no burning need to head home, I wandered over to the hard for a natter with Bert who I saw was painting the bottom of his boat which was sitting on some wooden blocks. My two dogs settled instantly alongside Otis and joined him in the pleasurable pastime of doing absolutely nothing.

It was low tide and we noticed a man out in the middle of Benfleet Creek poking around in the mud. It was not the usual place for bait diggers and his activities rather drew attention to someone who seemed to be intent on something in the mud. Every now and again he would poke a stick into the mud and then move off to a spot a few feet away. What could he be looking for we wondered, and we had a bit of a discussion as to whether or not there were shellfish in that spot and whether it would be wise to eat them if dug out so close to shore and possible sewage outlets.

But the man then seemed to find what he was looking for and shortly afterwards pulled up a length of chain, quite a long length as I recall, of about fifteen feet.

Though he must by then have been aware that he was being watched, the man produced a small hacksaw from his jacket and proceeded to cut the chain at a point a few links up from the mud. The effort involved in this took him over thirty minutes and it was clearly hard work, but eventually the job was done and the chain was cut loose and the man started to drag it ashore.

At that point Bert suddenly and unexpectedly went wild, and ran off down the boat ramp and struggle across the mud towards the man. A vigourous argument broke forth, with Bert using language I would not have thought a bank manager would have known and which would have made many a seaman blush. I saw the chain being placed back on the mud and the two men start to walk back to the hard.

Even Otis, not known for his speed and agility, jumped up to see what was happening and my two furry chums followed suit but all three dogs then lost interest and resumed their task of doing nothing.

I can't say what Bert said when he got back to the hard because it contained so many unprintable profanities, but I was given to understand that the offending gentleman had decided he needed some boat's chain to decorate a pool in his garden in a way he had seen on a television gardening programme and that, unfortunately for him, he had decided to use the mooring chain belonging to one of Bert's chums for that very purpose.

It was, of course, an outrage that the chap had decided to steal a mooring chain, though I tended to believe him when he said he thought it was merely an abandoned length of anchor chain. Clearly the man was shocked and extremely embarrassed at being discovered in the act and he freely identified himself to Bert, and later coughed up the cash for someone to go down and reconnect the chain with a new shackle.

It was, as the man said, a disappointing outing from which his original objective had not been fulfilled. Even worse, when Bert told him how cheaply such a chain could be obtained from the local ship chandler's, I thought he was going to weep.

We haven't seen that man again since, but Bert and I have a drink occasionally and often wonder whether he abandoned the idea of decorating his garden with anchor chain. We will never know.

Just as I will probably never know what treasures and horrors are buried in Two Tree Island.

Seven ~ Mayday! Mayday!

''Morning, Minnie!'
  'Good Morning, Gypsy!'
  'How is Monty this morning?'
  'Is Lucy being a good girl today?'
  'How are Daisy's stitches doing?'
  'Did Rizla and Baccy enjoy their holiday?'

These are not the greetings of people to other people, but of the dog owners to other people's dogs. Those of us that walk regularly on Two Tree Island usually pay more attention to the dogs than to their owners. At least, I am sure that is the case with me.

But, now and again, it is the dog that draws attention to its owner.

Take Jenny, for example.

Jenny was not just a beautiful, sleek white Labrador in the peak of condition, but a Guide dog as well, and from time to time her blind owner, accompanied by her sighted sister, Kate, would bring her down to Two Tree for some fun and relaxation out of her white leather working harness.

In time I came to know that the owner's name was Penny, a tall middle-aged lady who was born blind but who had a full and interesting life thanks to the Guide dogs she had owned. When asked one day why this one was called Jenny, she replied that the dog had that name when she acquired it and she did not want to change it.

So the alliterative Penny and Jenny, in company with Penny's sister were often to be seen out walking in the park, the two women arm in arm and the dog free of its harness and having the most wonderful time without restraint, but always keeping half an eye on her mistress.

I don't know what it is about Labradors, but they always seem irresistibly drawn to water as iron filings to a magnet. Eight times out of ten any time I see a Labrador on Two Tree Island, it is jumping into, splashing around or climbing out of water and thoroughly enjoying itself even in the depths of coldest winter. In this activity Jenny was no exception and the delight she got from playing, often with another of her canine acquaintances, was evident to anyone who saw her.

Someone once said to me that dogs and cats are incapable of play, but any pet owner knows this to be quite untrue. All of our dogs (and our cats, now I come to think of it) have indulged in play of various sorts throughout most of their lives. They have played on their own with balls in the garden, stalked imaginary foes or playfully chased with other dogs when out for walks and even just jumped around for joy in the grass, as is the case with little half-pint Ollie. All of our dogs have had their mad moments when, for no apparent reason other than for just pure fun, they have rushed wildly round and round the house or the garden.

And on this day Jenny was to be seen to be dripping wet, making the most of her freedom from her harness and happily running through puddles just for the sheer pleasure of it. As it happened, Jenny was not the only one out playing on Two Tree that day.

Those who know Two Tree Island may know of the model plane clubs that meet regularly down there to fly their planes.

Most of these aircraft have been meticulously handmade to scale and are amazingly accurate in their detailing. I've seen models of triplanes, biplanes, single-wing aircraft, jets and also helicopters down there performing acrobatics, flying in formation and occasionally having mock dogfights. There was even a chap I once saw trying, unsuccessfully I might add, to fly something which looked like a flying saucer.

These model aircraft obviously cost a fortune both in terms of money and in time, and their owners can usually be seen maintaining and polishing them and admiring each other's handicraft and flying skills.

The owners fly them - play with them seems somehow to be a disparaging term even though some of the owners might admit to be playing - around a prescribed area and within times laid down by the local council and, even to those of us with little interest in model aircraft, the flying antics are often quite absorbing as we walk.

But this was not the case with Jenny for, just as Piggy was to suffer years later, she was once bitten on the muzzle by a bumblebee and, to her, the noisy whine of the model aircraft merely signalled the existence of very large bumblebees, any one of which might at any time attack her.

So Jenny usually ran a wide circle away from the model aircraft field and rejoined Penny further along the path by the Tree Trunk Graveyard. In this way, she seemed to feel that she was well out of harm's way.

The owners of the model aircraft usually stay within their flying area, clearly marked by some signs, and also within their flying hours.

But there are always the rare exceptions; the clots who fly their models out of the flying area and just over the heads of the walkers, or those who take delight in dive-bombing the dogs. We curse those who abuse their privileges and make life difficult not only for the walkers and their dogs but also for their club colleagues who are content to operate within the club rules

It was a sultry summer afternoon and extremely hot and humid, with the air heavy with the scent of cut grass from the castle grounds and borne down to the island on a faint breeze. The sky was darkening, the birds had stopped twittering and the chances looked good that we would very shortly get another refreshing thunderstorm.

A couple of car-carriers were moored out in the Estuary waiting for a berth at their terminal upstream and the only sound that could be heard was the whining of a single model aircraft circling the club field.

It was a curious thing, but on this afternoon there seemed to be Labradors just about everywhere in the park. Other days one sees more border collies than other breeds, and on others the terriers seem to predominate. This is obviously just coincidence but I do sometimes wonder if there is some mysterious force at work and this was especially the case on the morning I once saw five Staffies.

However, I digress. The point is that on this afternoon there were a lot of Labradors in evidence and one of these was Jenny who was enjoying a walk out of her harness and, as I said before, happily plunging into the puddles left over from a rain shower the previous evening.

With Max and Ben trotting along slightly ahead of me I was walking along the rough middle track of the park and, as I climbed a hillock, I noticed that Penny and her sister Kate were walking arm in arm along the macadamised path. There was the buzz of a model aircraft and I looked for Jenny and saw that she was trotting over the grass in my direction, and knew that she would shortly swing back towards the Tree Trunk Graveyard to rejoin the main path and her owner.

The cause of her diversion was, of course, the noisy model aircraft she thought might be a large bumblebee and as I surveyed the scene the owner of the model obviously started to get bored and look for something more interesting to do.

He flew his plane in a wide circle roughly following the line of the main path and gradually bought it lower and lower until it was around six feet off the ground. Then, seeing me atop a hillock, he decided I would make a good dive-bombing target and aimed his plane at me.

But my path dipped down somewhat and so I and the dogs disappeared from sight for a short while and, as we crested the next hillock, I saw that the model aircraft had returned to flying very low over the hard path.

Not only was this a stupid thing to do, but it was a dangerous one as well for many of these aircraft have wingspans of three feet or more and are capable of causing major injuries if they crashed into someone.

And then, in the blink of an eye, it happened.

The plane came in again over the path, six feet off the ground, and this time it came perilously close to the heads of Penny and her sister Kate.

In the wink of an eye, as the plane drew level with the two women I saw Penny quickly raise her white stick and give the plane's starboard wing a glancing blow, sufficient to knock it off course.

The plane shot off towards the marsh and performed a dramatic last dive as its engine stalled and it plunged into the water and was gone from sight and sound.

I saw the two women laughing. I saw Jenny stop and look into the soundless sky and then, obviously deciding that the giant bumblebee had gone, run straight back to rejoin the two ladies, her tail wagging furiously.

And I saw the model's owner, who I later learned was nothing to do with either of the model plane clubs, running hard across the field towards the marsh in the vain hope of spotting the stricken aircraft in which he had doubtless invested much time and money, but which he had recklessly flown just moments before.

As Penny told me a few minutes later, 'I may be blind but my hearing is perfect, and I was determined to get that blighter if he gave me the chance!'

Which, unfortunately for him, he did.

Eight ~ Junk

Bearded Sam Walker was small in height but very muscular which, to those who knew him, was unsurprising given his occupation as one of our local cockle-fishermen.

He could be seen, when the tides were right, early in the morning with his two retrievers. He striding on ahead through the reserve on Two Tree Island, with the dogs snuffling around the fox and rabbit trails and chasing the occasional rabbit foolish enough to stay out of its burrow when these two bundles of energy were around.

I think it was close on twelve months before Sam said more than a brief, 'Morning!' when our paths crossed but, having effected that short introduction, there was a point when we started to natter on the occasions that we walked our dogs together. My little Ben was only a titch in doggy terms but he always regarded himself as being among the biggest of dogs and he got on very well with Sam's pair of retrievers and was always prepared to hunt and snuffle with them.

Sam was an interesting character and was a fund of stories about the local fishermen and their boats, and always delighted to chat about the good and bad times to those he got to know.

Clearly he loved the sea and his way of life. Tales of heaving boats in roaring winds and mountainous seas with the fishermen dangerously sliding around the decks, seemed to me to be a warning not to mess with small boats and to leave it to the professionals, a policy I have in any event always faithfully followed myself.

Indeed, Sam was highly critical of weekend yachtsmen who ventured into deep water without the proper training or the necessary equipment. He cited many instances of yachtsmen whose only radio or navigation equipment was a mobile phone, useless he said when more than a couple of miles offshore, and who then found themselves in difficulties. As for those yachties with GPS receivers, he thought these were about as useful as a cupful of cold water in a storm if their owners could not relate the bearings to a decent chart and he told me that many did not even go to the expense or bother of buying a proper chart. In both cases the frequent result was that a lifeboat had to be called out to assist the people back home when they got into difficulties.

There was one year when I saw more of Sam than was usual, and I remember asking him if he had retired from what was to me a dangerous and ill-paid occupation in favour of something less hazardous ashore.

But no. He was forced to be idle thanks to European Union legislation which cut fishing quotas and so reduced the amount of sea-time that he and his boat could legally have each year.

Not unnaturally, Sam was devastatingly rude about the Eurocrats and their interference in what he saw as a quintessentially English way of making a living. He was particularly bitter that the fishing boats still had to be regularly maintained and serviced even though their working time at sea had been reduced. 'Less time to make less money with ever-rising costs,' he complained. Since that day, Sam's problems with EU quotas have grown worse and so I see even more of him now.

It was towards the end of that particular year when I saw Sam one morning with only one dog. Both he and the remaining dog seemed much slower in their walk and from his brief response to my greeting Sam was clearly very depressed; even Ben understood that something seemed wrong and he approached the other dog with some caution.

I understood the reason when Sam told me that one of his dogs had died from an unknown illness, though he didn't know the exact cause since he wouldn't allow the vet to perform a post-mortem on the poor animal.

The loss of the dog affected Sam deeply and he quickly turned into a grouch that hardly had a good word to say about anyone or anything. It was a great shame seeing this grand chap turn sour.

Previously, Sam's only complaints had been about

inexperienced weekend yachtsmen and the hated bureaucrats of the EU. Now he complained about everything.

His chief complaint, and one with which I and many others had much sympathy, was about the mindless idiots that dump their rubbish around Two Tree Island.

Since a Council refuse tip free to residents of the borough, is sited just behind Leigh railway station, the people who dump their rubbish are either too mean to pay the small fee involved for those living outside the borough, are dumping stuff that ought not to be dumped indiscriminately anyway or are just plain lazy and inconsiderate.

Thus, over the years have we have seen garden and building rubbish deposited around the island along with cars, household appliances, old boats and even, on a couple of occasions, small caravans.

The rubbish deposited can be dangerous to inquisitive children and also to wild animals foraging for food and, in any event, are eyesores that are expensive to clear away.

Sam threatened to write to the Council on a number of occasions asking them either to put up a barrier to Two Tree at night or, alternatively, install closed-circuit television, but in the end he didn't bother as he figured no-one would take any notice.

The idea of closed-circuit television cameras appealed to me as they would provide the evidence to prosecute the people who despoil the island. It may well have started out to be the local rubbish tip, but it is now a wildlife refuge and a park giving much pleasure to many people throughout the year. But Sam may well have been right when he proffered the view that there were few votes to be won from stopping people dumping rubbish and there was little chance of any action resulting from a written complaint.

The dumping continued, as it still does today, and Sam got more and more angry on the subject and could often be seen riffling through the rubbish sacks in search of the evidence that might convict the people responsible.

He never found his evidence, and this is not surprising for I imagine that the people who come to the island at the dead of night to dump their unwanted rubbish take care that they leave no clues as to who they are.

I suppose there is an irony that a place which was built on rubbish and landfill now needs protecting from those who want to illegally dump their rubbish. There is also an irony in the fact that the toxic chemicals and other substances which were dumped there officially over so many years are even now leaching into the Estuary and creating a potential beach pollution problem further along the coast.

Nonetheless, Two Tree is one of the largest nature reserves in Essex and it deserves to be protected as such.

There was a year when Easter came at the end of March, a year that the government declared the start of British Summer Time on a morning when the frost lay thick on the deeply-frozen ground and a bitter wind was screaming up from the Estuary across Two Tree and turning the rigging of the boats into a noisy gamelan orchestra.

It was a morning when the resident pheasant was too cold to croak a warning as Ben and I took our walk in the reserve, and the few people out and about seemed supercharged as if anxious to get home and back close to their warm fires and a hot drink.

But it was the same morning, quite early, that I saw Sam with a new dog, a lovely exuberant, glossy-coated, young border collie, and I quickened my pace to learn where the new dog had come from. Ben shot off ahead of me to inspect the new addition to his circle of acquaintances.

Sam was in rare good form and proud to show off the new dog which, close to its mate and now joined by Ben, was foraging among the rabbit droppings and tearing off to investigate the various scent trails.

'Ain't 'e a beauty?' he asked, and I had to agree it was for it was a most magnificent animal and in very obvious good form.

'What's his name?' I asked.

'Junk!" came the answer.

Seeing the surprise on my face, Sam explained.

It seemed that a couple of weeks before, Sam had been looking over the wreck of an old car that had been abandoned in the car park close to the bridge. To his astonishment, this dog was tied to the car's bumper and clearly very cold and miserable.

'D'ye see?' Sam said. 'The dog weren't wanted either, 'an so I took him in. The best bit of rubbish I ever did see!'

Some people should not be allowed to own pets and it is beyond me how anyone could just dump a dog as being surplus to requirements and jettison it like a piece of unwanted rubbish, particularly a beautiful young dog such as this. But, on the other hand, this dog had the very good fortune to be found by Sam who was liberal in the love and attention he gave it.

There were two miracles that day.

The first was that Sam found a replacement dog that suited him and his other dog as an old glove fits a hand.

The second was that Sam returned to his usual cheerful self with scarcely a grumble - except, of course, for the EU fishing quotas and weekend yachtsmen.

Nine ~ Frankie and Charlotte

The vast majority of folk exercising themselves and their dogs on Two Tree Island have their animals firmly under control.

One such owner was Frankie Pullinger, a friendly athletic man in his mid-20s who would often be seen in the early mornings walking with his Irish Setter, Daisy, a lively animal with a beautiful, glossy mahogany coat.

You would first spot Daisy chasing after a short length of weighted rope that Frankie had thrown for her, which she would retrieve and drop at her master's feet and then bark for him to repeat the throw. (Would that little Ollie would learn this trick; he chases after balls, ropes and Frisbees, right enough, but he can't be bothered to bring them back to me!)

That Frankie and his dog were a team was beyond any dispute for when Daisy was not retrieving the rope she would usually be seen trotting quietly at his right side, though she sometimes joined other dogs for a short spell of doggie play but always with her master in sight. Daisy was an especial chum of Ben's and he always made a point of making a detour when he spotted her.

Frankie, who was usually unemployed, lived on the fringe of criminal society, though his friendly, chatty disposition gave no clue of this. But the frequent bargains he would offer people that he met hinted that he made his living as a fence, and his occasional absences strongly suggested that he might be enjoying a short stay as a guest of Her Majesty's Prison Service.

Odd bits of jewellery, along with watches, shoes, television sets, microwave ovens and the like showed that if he was not a fence, he had some extraordinary good trade contacts and could come up with some terrific bargains for those daft enough to get involved in buying things that came without guarantees or warranties.

The thing that mainly struck one about Frankie was not his forays into dubious retailing, but the amazing rapport he had with the dogs that he came across.

They just loved him and seemed to enjoy their encounters with him; you would see dogs chasing across the park at the first sight of him and, sad though it is to say, Frankie profited from this because the dog owners had little choice but to follow their dogs and, from time to time, be offered something cheap. Nonetheless, it was certainly true that Frankie had the gift of a special relationship with dogs.

When Frankie was not trying to persuade you to buy the latest so-called bargain, he would talk about dogs, a subject on which he was passionate and also very knowledgeable. He was a great believer in people taking the time and trouble to train their pets and was highly disapproving of those that didn't and who allowed their dogs to get out of control and do what they wished.

Indeed, I witnessed a few occasions when he gave sound advice to owners and even demonstrated his training techniques on the animals themselves. On such occasions, the dogs paid rapt attention to his commands and were seen to be obeying them with enthusiasm. Understandably, Frankie's reputation grew enormously from these encounters even though he sometimes used them to flog his dodgy wares rather than make some honest money by organising dog training classes of his own.

But, as I say, not all dog owners have their animals under control and one of these was Charlotte Sutton.

Charlotte was your archetypal English rose, a lovely slim young woman with a soft aristocratic accent but, one has to say it, not many brains. She was slow and ponderous in her thinking and also in her reactions to the things going on around her. Despite this, she had a charming personality and I confess to feeling sorry for her when I heard that she had been widowed shortly after her marriage when her husband was killed in a motorcycle accident.

Charlotte owned two long-haired spaniel crosses, Jet and Jasper, who were noisy menaces off the lead when they ran around completely out of control and blundered into other walkers and chased their dogs. It is probably fair to say that the dogs were basically boisterous, they never gave any suggestion of being dangerous.

The dogs' exuberant behaviour and their reluctance to come to heel or be put back on the lead was possibly the result of their being housebound for most of the day, for they were walked only in the mornings. Whatever the cause, Charlotte's inability to discipline them only made the situation worse and she and her dogs quickly developed a reputation for being bad news if encountered on Two Tree.

It was through the dogs that Frankie and Charlotte met.

It happened one crisp spring morning at low tide when the birds were foraging on the mud flats around the salt marsh.

As I came round by the boat hard accompanied by Ben and Piggy, Charlotte's dogs could be seen out on the mud. Close to a boat lying on its side, they had managed to corner a large gull which one of the dogs had injured. The bird was trying to defend itself and was hobbling around with a damaged leg and flapping its wings and making the most terrible screeching noise. Above and around flew other gulls shrieking and calling and feinting attacks on Jet and Jasper in an effort to divert their attention away from the injured gull.

The noise of the gulls and the barking of the two excited dogs attracted quite a bit of attention from the dog walkers in the vicinity and it was not long before Frankie put in an appearance.

Frankie exploded into a fury as the dogs closed in on the gull and eventually killed it. Rarely have I heard such bad language and so many gratuitous insults poured out by someone on the head of another, and the unhappy and deeply embarrassed Charlotte was weeping, most probably terrified that Frankie would attack her and vainly trying at the same time to gain some form of control over her dogs.

The damage was done. The gull had been killed in front of a number of people and Charlotte quickly found herself being ostracised by those who knew of the incident. Even worse, she took the brunt of Frankie's forcibly expressed views every time they passed close to each other.

A little while afterwards, Jet and Jasper were responsible for chasing the reserve's resident pheasant, fortunately without harming the bird, and as ill luck would have it Frankie was in the vicinity when it happened. Once again, Frankie tore into Charlotte with a torrent of abuse, bad language and advice as to how she should make a serious attempt to bring her two dogs under control.

But, wary of Frankie's strong views and the way in which he reinforced them, Charlotte did nothing. That is, until one bitterly cold winter's morning.

I was driving parallel to the railway line and just approaching the golf range before crossing the bridge over to the island. Ben and Piggy were in the back of the car and impatient to get on with their morning walk.

In the distance I could see a tree that the day before had been completely bare of leaves and yet which seemed suddenly and unaccountably to have blossomed overnight with huge black and white blooms; the tree was covered in them. As I drew closer, I could see with some surprise that the blooms were in fact around forty or so magpies.

Close to the tree were Frankie and Charlotte and their dogs were sitting quietly on the frost-covered grass nearby.

I stopped the car and, leaving Ben and Piggy inside, quietly got out to take a look at the amazing sight of a tree that contained so many birds. They were sitting completely motionless and quite silent. The effect was quite striking, eerie almost, and reminiscent of Alfred Hitchcock's film 'The Birds.'

Usually the magpies are a noisy chattering lot, fidgeting about and bickering constantly when in a group. Yet this morning they seemed to be acting as if they had been frozen to the branches. Not a head turned at the three of us; we might just as well have been invisible.

But Jasper, impatient with an inactivity not prompted by him, started to bark in protest at the delay. At this signal, the birds flew off in the direction of the castle. This was no phased withdrawal, for the birds took flight in an instant and in one graceful uniform movement.

It was a strange sight and one that I have not seen since, but I was glad to have seen it.

And Frankie and Charlotte seemed pleased to have seen it also for, as we went on our way, the two seemed to be talking quite civilly to each other.

Indeed, as the weeks passed it became clear that Frankie had softened his attitude towards Charlotte and, from the reformed behaviour of her dogs, it was clear that Frankie had worked his charm on them as well. From that time on, Jet and Jasper were happily under control and attentive to the commands given by their mistress and, on occasion, by Frankie also.

Their romance blossomed and, after some months, I understood that Frankie had moved into Charlotte's house and, as I discovered a little while later, he found employment in a local boarding kennels where he also did some work as a dog trainer.

You'd have thought that these two people would have got married and lived very happily ever after.

But no, there is no fairy-tale ending to this tale.

Frankie lost his job at the kennels, returned to his old life and, when not enjoying three free meals a day and a warm and comfortable prison cell, can still be counted upon to offer a dodgy deal from time to time.

As for Charlotte, I heard that she married an army officer who wanted a wife with looks and not brains. And, when she accompanied her new husband on a posting abroad, Jet and Jasper became surplus to their requirements and were separated and rehomed.

But they had, at least, been trained to behave properly.

Ten ~ The Flasher Foiled

Like many other such places, Two Tree Island attracts its fair share of eccentrics and other strange people.

There is, for example, the middle-aged man who used to appear extremely early on Thursday mornings in winter dressed in boots, battle fatigues, helmet and an army-type backpack. This harmless soul had charge of an imaginary body of men who he marched around at a fairly strenuous pace, barking out orders and reprimanding slackers in the manner and vocal volume you expected from cruel Sergeant Majors of decades ago.

One is used to seeing walkers or joggers belting at top speed round the island but this fellow came as a bit of a shock the first time round, for you expected him to be accompanied by a company of sweating soldiers. Alas, if they existed, they existed only in the man's mind but nonetheless the initial effect could be startling.

There are many others.

The man who very occasionally sleeps in his saloon car, again only in wintertime, and who neatly places his shoes and socks underneath the car to air overnight is another example. Would that I had the courage to ask him if his wife throws him out of the house from time to time, for there seems to be no other reason for his sporadic appearances. I wonder too what he would do if a fox or a dog stole one of his shoes or a sock one night.

Then there is the fellow who some time ago used to be seen training his gun-dog. Kitted out with tweeds, plus-fours, deerstalker hat and with a canvas bag slung over one shoulder, he used to be seen blundering around the undergrowth in the reserve trying to get his dog used to the idea of retrieving the birds he shot, furiously blowing on a dog-whistle all the while. Quite acceptable behaviour one might think - ignoring for the moment the fact that he was hunting in a protected nature reserve! - until one came to understand that this man had neither a gun nor a dog.

But, as they say, it takes all sorts to make a world.

Two of these sorts were the lovely ladies who, because of their Cockney accents and extreme sense of humour, I quickly christened Gert and Daisy.

Gert and Daisy were two widows who, for daily companionship and I suppose also protection from the occasional weirdo, met each other in the car park at the same time every morning and afternoon and walked their black Labradors. These were a great favourite of Soda's who was normally very timid and cautious in the company of larger dogs.

Of extremely cheery disposition, these two ladies had a very high profile since they formed an obvious pocket of boisterous noise as they walked around the island's park. The two dogs were firm friends also and could be seen splashing about the puddles, playing happily together, racing off after imaginary rabbits and each other as the mood took them and sometimes accompanied by Soda when the mood took her.

To those who met them, the one feature of these two ladies to stick in the mind was their sense of humour which was extremely earthy and very, very sharp. And, chatting to them one morning, I was reminded of the Gert and Daisy of those very far-off days when we used to listen to the wireless and use our imaginations, rather than sit in front of the idiot-box with our brains numbed.

Anyway, I digress yet again.

There was a summer when reports started to circulate about a flasher making an occasional afternoon appearance on the island and, in a world weary of hearing horror stories of sex attacks and a newly-publicised paedophile interest in children, quite a few folk became alarmed.

I suppose there was an inevitability about such strange behaviour surfacing on the island. But not for long, for it was Gert and Daisy who fixed the problem, at least insofar as Two Tree was concerned.

It was a Saturday afternoon and a very hot one indeed and the island was full of families out and about enjoying themselves, wandering the paths, picnicking, walking their dogs and enjoying what little breeze came in off the estuary. Indeed, I was walking the reserve with Soda and so heard myself firsthand what happened to Gert and Daisy in the park on the other side of the island.

As I heard the tale from their lips in the car park shortly after it happened, they were strolling round the metalled path close to the area we call the Tree Trunk Graveyard, which is where the local council dumped the stumps of trees felled during the hurricane of a few years ago.

As usual, Gert and Daisy were gossiping and laughing about nothing in particular and their two dogs were snuffling around nearby.

Without warning, a clean-shaven middle-aged man sprang out from among the tree trunks and, adopting a stance that he might have imagined to resemble Superman descending from the sky, opened his shabby raincoat wide and exposed himself.

He was, it appears, your archetypal old-fashioned, cartoon-character flasher and, apart from a red and blue Superman tee-shirt wore only short trouser legs fastened with elastic just above calf level. Yellow socks and black shoes were his only other form of clothing.

Of course, he looked utterly ridiculous and, instead of being shocked, Gert and Daisy burst into uncontrolled paroxysms of wild and hysterical laughter.

The man seemed surprised and startled that his appearance hadn't achieved the desired effect - whatever that was supposed to be - because he drew forth a string of questions and comments from the two ladies who wanted to know if he was poor and couldn't afford a full set of trousers, where had he escaped from, had he lost his Mummy and so on and so forth.

Worse still for him, he was barraged with comments about the diminutive size of his member and, among many other caustic comments, given advice on how he might improve it and how it might get bigger when he reached puberty and that, in any event, it looked as if it badly needed ironing.

The man's reaction to this fusillade of wit was one of utter confusion and, instead of moving quickly away, he was transfixed to the spot. Which was a mistake.

For Daisy's dog, out of curiosity, quietly came up behind the flasher and sniffed his bare backside with a cold, wet nose. And the man's sudden alarmed reaction to that, and the screech he made because of it, so frightened Gert's dog that it promptly jumped up at him and ripped off most of his raincoat.

The flasher got his brain into gear at that point and made a run for it, clutching what little was left of his raincoat and, with Gert and Daisy's shrill laughter and acid comments still ringing in his ears, made off at top speed for the car park and, presumably, the safety of his own car and then a get-a-way.

Several astonished people saw this poor demented man, running as fast as he could go. Red-faced and stark naked except for a Superman tee-shirt and trouser-leg bottoms flapping over his yellow socks and clutching what seemed to be a rag in one hand.

Needless to say, he has not been seen again.

But Gert and Daisy have and, if you ask them, they will happily tell you the tale of the day they foiled the Two Tree Island Flasher.

Eleven ~ Boris, The Money Dog

Though it is a statement of the blindingly obvious, dogs come in all shapes and sizes, and what is an attractive dog to one person can appear to be an ugly one to another.

But, in respect of one dog, anyone who saw it would agree without any reservation whatsoever that Boris the bulldog was the ugliest brute that they ever saw.

There can be no shadow of a doubt that Boris was ugly.

For a start he only had one eye, the result of an accident when he blundered into a moving car when he was a puppy. But unlike most of the bulldog breed, Boris was misshapen with folds of flesh where none should have been and folds of skin missing where some should have shown.

An amiable, though terrifically and grossly overweight, animal Boris was prone to making a slow but friendly charge on anyone he encountered during his twice-daily walks on Two Tree Island and was quite capable of knocking over anyone who didn't spot or hear him coming in time. Those of us that knew him quickly discovered the trick of side-stepping his amiable lunges, though I have seen some folk understandably get quite agitated when charged by the old fellow.

The one distinguishing feature of Boris, as some of us came to know, was that he could smell money.

How he did it with only one working eye partly obscured by a roll of fatty flesh, no-one quite understood, but it was a fact that every now and again he presented his mistress with a coin or a bank note. On rare occasions he even found small items of jewellery such as a cufflink or an earring.

You might think that the owner of this overweight and ugly pooch would be a burly man with a healthy outdoor occupation and tattooed pectorals to match. But no, his owner was as slight and frail as Boris was heavy and exuberant.

Caroline Tyzack was a middle-aged single lady who easily

gave the impression that a puff of wind would blow her over. Yet this seemingly frail woman was more than capable of controlling Boris when she had to, and the two were clearly devoted to each other.

I never knew Caroline's background, yet her accent and demeanour suggested she came from a genteel family that might have fallen on hard times. Indeed, Caroline's clothes indicated that she was living in impoverished circumstances and the odd conversational comment gave warning that she sometimes had a tough time making ends meet. I suspected that much of Caroline's income went on supporting the grotesque but amiable Boris, and so it was perhaps appropriate that the odd present of cash from this amazingly ugly animal gave some little relief to his mistress.

I first encountered Boris when, deep in thought one afternoon and not concentrating on my surroundings, a fifty-something-pound thump in the back of my legs from Boris bought me crashing sharply to the ground and occasioned not a little surprise to me as well as to Soda who was always cautious of dogs that were larger than her.

The fall was a surprise but did me no harm and it was through this that I got to know Caroline and also appreciate the finer attributes, for there were a few, of her exuberant and friendly pet. Now and again we would walk together and, apart from getting enjoyment hearing about Caroline's wide range of interests, I saw for myself over the years how Boris seemed to smell out the odd coin or bank note and bring it to her feet with a loud grunt and a self-satisfied look on his one-eyed ugly face.

There was one morning when Boris found a German mark coin, another when he found a fifty pence piece and yet another when he snuffled out a five-pound note. There were many other such instances.

It was really quite amazing, and how he managed this useful trick was a complete mystery. Sometimes the things Boris found would be discovered in the long grass and whether the animal could smell their presence or just blundered across them, Caroline didn't know.

Though I get much enjoyment from walking around Two Tree, there are the odd occasions when I do wonder whether I wouldn't have been better off staying in bed.

There was one such winter morning when Soda and I struggled around the park against a stiff biting wind blowing in off the estuary. It was a winter when we actually had some proper snow, and the warm cosiness of my house gave no warning as to how unbelievably cold it was in the world outside until we stepped out into it first thing.

Nonetheless, it was obvious that it was cold before we left the house and so this particular morning, I put Soda's warmest coat on her and muffled myself up as well.

I was heavy with a streaming cold and it seemed unfair not to let Soda have some exercise and enjoy the scents she encounters along the way or to inflict the duty on my wife, and so off we went into a wind that seemed to me that morning to be closely related to Antarctica's Katabatic.

We set off round the metalled path of the park in the direction of the Sea Scout hut with the wind screaming through the rigging of the boats stored on their blocks on the hard nearby. There was a moment when I thanked heaven that it was at least dry and then cursed my unspoken thought as it started to snow heavily. Within minutes a veritable blizzard was in progress and all views were blotted out by the fluffy white stuff.

Soda seemed not to mind rain or snow and only reacted to the wind with a degree of puzzlement when it came at her from behind and ruffled her feathery tail. At such times, as on this morning, she stopped and looked hard in a vain attempt to discover the invisible force that was interfering with her.

We had reached the hut and I had stopped for the umpteenth time to blow my snuffly nose when the faint sound of Boris pounding up the by now snow-covered path behind me caused me to brace myself against the inevitable friendly lunge. In the event, I managed to side-step him.

Caroline, heavily muffled against the weather, was coming up behind him and beaming all over her face. 'He did a grand job this morning!' she said with steaming breath. 'He's found me a twenty pound note!'

As soon as I put my hankie back into my empty pocket, I realised that it was my note that Boris had found and that it must have fallen out when I grabbed my hankie.

I said nothing.

I had no immediate need for the money but I knew that Boris, the ugliest dog in the world, and his mistress would be enjoying a meat dinner later on that bitterly cold day and that the cigarettes I was going to buy on the way home, but would not be able to taste, could wait until later.

Twelve ~ Zebedee

I can't say that there is a great deal of animal life on Two Tree Island, but what little that exists down there is quite interesting to see.

The reserve is, of course, dominated by the rabbits that can be seen grazing first thing most mornings. Some of them seem to enjoy grooming themselves in the middle of the paths where they can easily spot folk and animals coming, and I am often surprised at how close they allow one to get to them before they lollop away back into the undergrowth.

Doubtless because of the rabbit population, there are two or three resident foxes and these are usually seen only when they trot across the paths and disappear into the bushes in front of you. They too are quite used to the presence of humans on the island; indeed, on one occasion a young fox sat on his haunches and patiently watched Ollie and I walking towards him and, to Ollie's absolute astonishment, only ambled off into the undergrowth when we were within six or seven feet of it.

There is also an abundance of voles, busy little creatures that scurry onto the crown of the paths, change their minds and then rush back the way along the way they came. Their cousins, the water voles, can sometimes be seen in the ponds on the reserve and in the reservoir by the salt marsh, as are water rats from time to time. On the odd occasion I have also briefly spotted a stoat or a weasel, they seem to be yet more creatures that are always in a desperate rush and hurry.

To my knowledge, there are no badgers or squirrels; possibly the railway line, cultivated fields and the creek act as a break preventing them from entering the island. Though I have yet to see one, notices give clear warning that there are adders in the park and I know one young woman whose dog was bitten by one and had to be hospitalised as a result.

The rabbits seem to avoid the park, and I assume that this is because there is less topsoil over the compacted rubbish and it is more difficult for them to dig their burrows, though their slow and gradual approach towards the park can be detected annually by the advance shown by their droppings. And perhaps because of this and the number of ground-nesting birds that reside there, I have seen foxes around the park foraging for a snack.

There was one occasion when I saw a fox trot quite happily around the metalled path of the park, though it has to be admitted that it was a tame one rescued when quite young and at the end of an expanding leash.

On that particular morning, Soda and I were in the company of Julia and her King Charles Spaniel which sported the less than regal name of Charlie.

Julia was a petite and trim young woman in, I would guess, her mid 40's and was a doctor's receptionist locally. With a bright and cheerful disposition, she was a pleasant companion when out walking and I heard much about the various trips that she and her husband had with a group of like-minded friends who gave themselves an autumn break each year, visiting places such as Rome, Florence and Amsterdam.

It was good to hear of her annual adventures with this group, and I sometimes wished that I could have been part of it for they seemed to make the most of the bars and restaurants they visited in their travels though they did occasionally seem to find time to visit the main sites of interest also.

The morning we saw the tame fox, Charlie was bouncing around with as much animation as his mistress, though he got not so much as a glance from Soda who, as usual with most of the dogs that she encountered on Two Tree, ignored him completely. So far as she was concerned, Charlie simply did not exist.

That particular morning, Julia was herself in exceptional form having just returned from a trip to Lake Garda with her group of friends. I heard about the appalling wet weather they had for the complete week and how they had carried on as normal and didn't let it spoil their fun or limit their sightseeing. Indeed, from what Julia said, the rain positively seemed to encourage their attendance in the local bars and restaurants and I got the impression that they didn't spend a great deal of time out of doors during the whole, gently alcoholic, time.

This group of friends must have been unique for they seemed to go away together at least once a year and, to be truthful, I was not a little jealous.

And then Julia disappeared and I was not to see her until three or four weeks afterwards when I came across her walking slowly round the park on her own and looking very dejected indeed. Charlie was not in sight and I soon learned that he had got out of the house one afternoon and had not been seen since. There was a possibility that he had been stolen as sometimes does happen in these days when most things seem to have a price attached to them.

Julia was, of course, heartbroken at his disappearance and despite notices posted on the trees and telephone poles all over the district, phone calls to the police and visits to the various animal rescue centres, Charlie was never seen again.

I had much sympathy for Julia, for it is terrible when an animal sickens and dies and it must be even worse not knowing what happened to your friend and pet, and whether it has been adopted by someone as a stray, knocked down and killed or even stolen.

The effect on Julia was clearly devastating and her bubbly personality had taken a nose-dive. Now and again she came down to the island to see if Charlie had gone there, but he had not and eventually she stopped coming down as she found the place just too depressing without Charlie.

About six months later, Julia reappeared on the island with a new animal, Zebedee, and I was glad to see that her vibrant personality had returned in full measure. I had missed her company and here she was again, full of stories about her latest trip and of sessions in restaurants and bars that made me extremely envious.

On an expanding lead and harness, Zebedee walked sedately alongside his mistress stopping now and again to sniff a blade of grass or to investigate the marking left by the last dog over a particular spot.

He walked regally, tail fully erect like the mast of a ship and with pointed alert ears. Now and again he nuzzled Julia's leg in an appreciative suggestion that he was enjoying his walk.

Sometimes Julia asked it a question and the animal would give a low growl or a whine depending upon its mood and the response.

It was extraordinary how the two seemed to be having their own conversation, Julia making comment or asking a question and Zebedee responding instantly and enthusiastically.

Indeed, over the coming weeks, Zebedee became such a novelty on the island that various people would stop and pet it and talk to it. Zebedee quite liked the attention he got and was more than happy to comment on the issue of the moment or give his view on the state of the weather or on a dog that seemed to be less than under control and which was in danger of becoming a nuisance. On such occasions, a left paw would be raised in a threatening manner, a bit of a low growl given and the boisterous animal would subside in deference to one whose personal authority over the canine world was clearly beyond any question or doubt.

Very unusually, Soda took to Zebedee instantly and the two often nuzzled each other affectionately as we walked around the park. It was Zebedee who had the upper hand though, and Soda clearly deferred to the smaller and younger animal.

Which was a little bit of a surprise - because Zebedee was a cat. A beautiful, sleek Siamese cat. An A1, top-drawer, first-prize cat and very well aware of his own superiority.

Julia had at long last gone looking for another dog but had spotted Zebedee in one of the animal shelters and had instantly fallen in love with it. Julia believes with all her heart that Zebedee had fallen in love with her, but is prepared to admit that the truth might have been that Zebedee had spotted a soft touch coming a mile off and had turned his charm on her.

Either way, Zebedee took up residence with Julia and had an extremely comfortable life with her.

It seems that one afternoon, Zebedee followed Julia on a visit to the local butcher's shop and, wondering if he would like to walk more often as some Siamese cats do, Julia bought him a harness.

And the rest is history.

So in addition to the rabbits, the foxes, the voles, the weasels and the stoats that scurry around Two Tree Island, you might well see a very superior Siamese cat trotting alongside his mistress.

But not on Fridays, for that is when Julia does her shopping and Zebedee has to stay safely indoors at home on those days.

'Soda'

Thirteen ~ The Biter Bit

Though a number of local radio broadcasts on wildlife subjects have been made from Two Tree Island, I don't think anyone has ever made a film about or on it. This is a great shame since, to my mind at any rate, there is much of interest to be seen on and around it.

So far as I know, the closest the island has ever come to a film unit is when one of the television companies used the southern car park and boat hard to position its support units when they were filming an episode of a detective series close by in Old Leigh. At that time, the catering trucks were an absolute magnet for Soda who was always interested in any source of a titbit, and that was undoubtedly true of many of the other dogs who passed by at the film crew feeding times.

It is not only the island and its feathered and furry inhabitants and visitors that would make a good documentary. We have quite a few humans that would make a good subject for a television programme.

Take Grumpy for example.

We never knew what his real name was, he was just called Grumpy because no-one ever saw him in anything other than a foul, bad-tempered mood. He was an odd sort of chap that oftentimes would greet anyone foolish enough to bid him good day with a raised two fingered salute from a skeletal hand and even sometimes a curt and surly, 'Sod off!'

A thin, grey and cadaverous-looking man in his mid-50s, Grumpy had a gentle shaggy dog of indeterminate origin that was only ever allowed to travel in the back of his rusting open truck.

This long-suffering dog received much sympathy from the Two Tree's dog walkers, for Grumpy was constantly shouting at and browbeating the poor animal for no good reason. Indeed, there were occasions when Soda and I were walking in the reserve that we could hear Grumpy in the park shouting at his dog and it made me wonder why a man like that bothered owning a pet that, in any event, deserved better treatment.

But it was not only the cowering dog that usually drew our attention to Grumpy but also his truck, for he was suspected, without any solid proof I might add, of being one of those inconsiderate people who regularly fly-tip rubbish in the car park near the reserve.

Suspicions were raised by Grumpy's sudden appearances on Two Tree Island with a truck load of hard core or other builders' rubbish which, when one next saw him a little while later, would have disappeared.

A number of us quietly kept an eye on the old devil, but we never caught him in the act of fly-tipping even though we strongly suspected him of it.

Then it was the end of May, and the time when the spring blossoms were giving way to the summer flowers and their various scents were heavy in the still air.

I was taking an early morning stroll with Soda and noting that the odd patch of rape was springing up amongst the lush nettles, the spindly cow parsley and the withering remains of the bluebells. As we progressed around the reserve, blackbirds called out their warnings of our approach and were answered by the croak of a couple of crows and the repetitive cry of a lone cuckoo.

In the background, I heard the faint sputterings of a vehicle that I knew to be Grumpy's and I turned away from where he was likely to be heading. He was not a pleasant man to encounter under normal circumstances, and if he was going to do some fly-tipping I did not want to be seen by him to be around when he did it.

As it happened, the commotion of some ducks squabbling on the pond drew my attention away from Grumpy and his activities, and Soda and I took a turn in that direction and then slowly wandered back along the sea wall by the reservoir.

The faint thrum-thrum of a ship's engines grew louder and presently a large cruise ship appeared from the direction of

Southend Pier and disappeared behind the silhouette of Canvey Island on its way up to London.

Soda and I had a good walk and we stopped now and again to look at the gulls foraging among the mud on the seaward side of the path for food, and a duck shepherding her ducklings into the centre of the reservoir and away from a rabbit innocently grazing on the edges.

As we came closer to the car park, we could hear the commotion created by a small group of people seen in the distance. I heard the unmistakable sounds of an argument but, at the same time, could also hear the sound of laughter and was highly curious as to what might be going on.

When we came within sight of the car park there was Grumpy and his truck, a police car with its lights flashing, a couple of police officers and five or six bystanders along with their dogs.

Grumpy, arms wildly gesticulating, was red in the face and stridently arguing with one of the police officers. The other officer was quietly talking to the amused bystanders who were clearly enjoying the occasion.

My curiosity was boundless and I made a detour that would bring me past the group, and I quickly learned with some amusement that the police were questioning Grumpy about the present whereabouts of a load of builders' rubbish that had, an hour before he had turned off the main road and on to Two Tree Island, been seen by them to be resting on the back of his truck. A load of hardcore, with the dust still faintly rising in the air and suggesting that it had not long since been dumped, was not far from where the group was standing.

It was also clear that it was not only being questioned about the dumped builders' rubbish that Grumpy was upset about, but the presence of a large refrigerator that was now resting on the back of his truck, and heavy enough to lower its back wheels on their rusting springs.

That Grumpy had been caught, almost red-handed, in the act of fly-tipping was one thing, and he seemed almost to be happy to confess to that crime. What seemed to be upsetting him more was not that he was going to have to clear up the mess he had just created, find a place to dump it legally and ultimately be fined.

No. What was really making him very, very mad, and creating much interest among the small crowd of amused onlookers that had gathered, was that a person or persons unknown had dumped their old refrigerator on the back of his truck while he had been walking his dog!

There was a poetic justice somehow in this case of the biter being bit. On top of his woes, he was now going to have to pay to dump someone else's refrigerator and that is what really upset him. Obviously, no-one ever owned up to the deed, but you have to admit it was a slick one. Ironic even.

Grumpy hasn't been seen on Two Tree since then. And for that, we are all very grateful.

The thing that sticks in my mind from that day was the old dog of indeterminate origin, for I saw the poor old fellow wagging his tail and looking happy. And with good reason.

For, once the police understood that the dog was normally carried on the back of the truck unharnessed, Grumpy received another warning.

And the result of that was that we believe the dog of indeterminate origin was allowed to sit up front on the passenger seat from that day on!

Fourteen ~ The Dragon Brooch

I have never been a lover of poodles, which seem to me to be effeminate creatures bred to mainly ornament their owners. I am, however, quite prepared to admit that many people do not share this view and firmly believe that their thoroughbred poodles are the aristocrats of the doggie world.

Ron Perkins was one of these; he was the proud owner of a highly-coiffeured pink poodle whose coat was shaped into the ridiculous pom-poms one sometimes sees on these animals in dog shows and which had been given the equally ridiculous name of Marmaduke.

Ron, quite honestly, was a pain in the butt. He was arrogant and overbearing, and one of those self-opinionated chaps that knew everything about all and anything, and who could not resist topping any tale or story with a better one of his own. He was, in short, highly irritating.

Ron was a retired jeweller and dabbled in making pieces of silver jewellery of his own design which he would show, and sometimes try to sell at outrageous prices, to anyone he met while walking Marmaduke on Two Tree Island.

The problem was that the jewellery he made was heavy and clumsy and, because of this, very unattractive. Consequently he sold very little of it, as he admitted to me one afternoon in an unguarded moment. You could see why, for many of his brooches had jagged sharp edges - a design feature he called them - which were positively dangerous.

Over time, I began to feel not a little sorry for Ron who, though I never saw his wife, I believed to be married.

Ron, despite his opinions and his brashness, was one of life's losers but he was one of those who never recognised it and charged on regardless; a fortunate quality perhaps in someone such as he you might think.

You would see him walking around Two Tree on the lookout for someone to flog a piece of silver to, while Marmaduke tiptoed around the place trying not to get his paws wet or be pounced on by a proper dog such as one of the many Labradors and collies you see boisterously playing in the ponds and puddles and rushing around with all the exuberance of their breeds. You would know when Marmaduke was in the area, for you could hear a silver miniature cowbell tinkling away as he teetered and tottered about.

Now and again you would see Ron in the distance stop someone, usually an unsuspecting stranger, who could soon be seen trying to tear himself away from this odd man trying to sell his awful jewellery like a failed wartime spiv.

Then one day Ron had an idea that even I thought might work for him.

He read in a newspaper about a man who designed an expensive piece of jewellery to, if I recall correctly, a peacock design and which he buried somewhere. Then he wrote a book which gave clues as to where the peacock brooch was buried.

Ron decided to do the same thing and spent months designing a brooch in the shape of an oriental dragon. He showed me the design and, much later on, the brooch itself and I have to admit that, for once, it was quite a nice piece that he said was worth over £1,000.

In fact, it was quite interesting hearing over the long winter months one year how the design evolved, for it was based on a print of a Chinese Imperial Dragon. As he worked on the design, he gave much thought to the tooling and polishing of it and the final pattern was a much simplified version though still highly evocative of the original print, even to one of the creature's claws holding a small pearl.

Ultimately, the piece was made and I will be honest enough to admit that I was privileged to be given a private viewing of it when, one morning, Ron unwrapped it from a piece of tissue paper and showed it to me.

With eyes of small rubies, and fangs and claws made of tiny delicate pieces of ivory and holding one bright lustrous pearl, the piece was just beautiful. Clearly a lot of craftsmanship and time had gone into it and I could not help but wonder why, if he was able to create such a wonderful thing, that the rest of the stuff he produced and rarely sold was so crude and awful.

Having made the brooch, Ron now turned his mind to where he would hide it and how he would insert the clues to its resting place in a book that he would write and which would pay for the cost of the brooch and turn a profit as well.

Occasionally, he would ask my views on whether a triangulation on Hadleigh Castle and the tower of St. Clement's Church might be too easy a final clue and, if so, how he could obscure the directions without making the various preceding clues meaningless or unnecessary. It was a problem even I had to admit and, as the summer turned to autumn and then into the next winter, Ron had yet to work the details out.

But he had decided where to bury the brooch and, though he would not let me in on the secret, he did admit that it would be somewhere on Two Tree. On a number of occasions, I saw him prospecting a possible site for the brooch and I eventually became fairly certain that it would be in the reserve at the eastern end of the island facing the Estuary and the Kent coast.

He would not be drawn on when he was going to bury the brooch but seemed keen, despite my earnest advice to the contrary, to do it fairly soon.

Ron now started to be extremely secretive and I guessed, correctly as it turned out much later on, that he had almost completed his book and the series of clues that would step by step lead the readers to the place where the brooch was buried.

That winter was a fairly mild one and as it turned into spring, Ron admitted one morning that he had buried the brooch in a small blue Chinese porcelain pot about eighteen inches below ground level, and that he was about to send his manuscript to a publisher who had become interested in his project.

I did wonder if burying the brooch at that point might not have

77

been precipitate, but Ron was quite confident that it could not be found without the clues he had put in his book.

Much of Two Tree is made of compacted rubbish over which was thrown a layer of topsoil. Now and again, bits of crockery and other household rubbish come to the surface when rabbits and other small animals turn the ground over.

Nowhere on Two Tree is the evidence that the land was reclaimed from being a rubbish tip as good as the reserve at the eastern end, and much rubbish was to be seen just laying on the surface.

I say was.

That spring some children, as I supposed, decided it would be fun to set light to some of the rubbish, and the fire they set lasted for many weeks and well on into the summer when the amount of smouldering land producing clouds of acrid smoke became such a nuisance that the Fire Brigade were asked to come down and deal with it.

It took the firemen a couple of days to settle the fire, which continued to smoulder on in a half-hearted sort of way for two or three weeks afterwards. At that time, the area affected resembled a series of moon craters where the top soil had collapsed into the spaces left by the burnt material.

Shortly afterwards, the Council sent in some tipper trucks with more topsoil and some days later a bulldozer was sent in to level out the whole area and make it look a bit more presentable. Indeed, more presentable it looked and within a few weeks the ferns and grasses and even some small bushes were seen to be re-establishing themselves and covering the area with a green and lush foliage.

When the fire occurred, Ron was on his annual eight-week visit to relatives in Australia and Marmaduke had been staying with Ron's brother somewhere in Suffolk. So when I mentioned the fire to him on his return from his holiday one morning, the shock on his suddenly blood-drained face was very evident.

There and then, he insisted on walking over to the devastated site which by then had been bulldozed flat and which was now beginning to be covered by fresh greenery. But the three fruit trees that had been there before the fire had disappeared, either burned or bulldozed.

Ron was inconsolable, for all trace of the place where he had buried the dragon brooch had now disappeared and, as I then understood it, with the disappearance of the fruit trees, any chance of anyone making a triangulation to the spot where he had buried his brooch. Besides which, the bulldozer might have moved the pot to another spot or even broken it and, in addition, it might even now languish some feet below the new surface.

Over the next few weeks, Ron was seen to be digging in various spots on the eastern end of Two Tree but, as he made clear to me, without any success. As for the book, that was abandoned.

Poor old Ron. If he had not been so keen to bury the brooch before the book was produced, all might have been well. But, as they say, that is the utterly useless power of hindsight.

Not long afterwards, Ron moved to Suffolk and was not seen again.

Leaving a rather nice dragon brooch said to be worth over £1,000 buried somewhere at the eastern end of Two Tree Island.

Fifteen ~ Secrets

Two Tree Island undoubtedly hides many secrets.

The Warden may show you an overgrown spot where the wild bee-orchids grow or point out the nest in which a kestrel has lately laid her eggs but, since these spots and others like them become known, by definition they can no longer be classed as being secret. On one occasion the body of a woman was discovered in the burned-out wreck of a car but, in the fullness of time, the details behind that murder became public knowledge and were no longer the secret they were when the incident was first discovered.

In the main, the island keeps its secrets to itself. I'd like to know, for instance, where Ron Perkins' dragon brooch finally ended up but I doubt if it will ever be found, and so that will be one secret that will be kept. I'd also like to know about the bench that I came to call Dusty's Log, for that is another secret that the island will keep to itself now that Dusty himself is dead.

As late summer gives way to the autumn and the mist settles low over the island, giving it the appearance of a painted oriental landscape in which the trees and other features fade in and out of the picture, the island takes on a secretive atmosphere of its own. The mist deadens any sound save that of the mournful ships' sirens groaning in the estuary, and even the muffled scampering of the rabbits through the undergrowth of the reserve as you draw close is heard but faintly.

Though it may be my imagination, it is at such times that the island seems to attract people who are themselves of a secretive disposition and, perhaps, I am one of them. It may be my fancy, but Dusty Miller was one such person who I only ever seemed to see on misty mornings.

Dusty used to be a librarian somewhere in London and after he was widowed he moved down to Leigh where he acquired Bess, a black mongrel. The two could be seen shuffling round Two Tree at a fairly sedate pace but had the irritating habit of popping up where you least expected them. You would see them in front of you close to the Tree Trunk Graveyard disappearing into the mist, and a few minutes later they would disconcertingly reappear behind you at some other spot.

It seemed impossible to establish much of a rapport with Dusty, who was one of those solitary types who have little conversation except on subjects which interest them. And for years, insofar as I was concerned, Dusty appeared to have no conversation or interests whatsoever and we barely exchanged greetings as our paths crossed on Two Tree.

Then one year, I had just returned from a trip to Egypt and was wearing one of those touristy tee-shirts with a representation of Tutankhamun's mummy mask on it, when Dusty spotted it and, to my surprise, we were soon having a lengthy in-depth conversation about ancient Egypt, a subject on which Dusty was extremely knowledgeable.

As it happens, ancient Egypt is an interest of mine also and it was not long before we developed a warm relationship as we sometimes walked in the mornings and discussed various theories about the purpose of the pyramids and how they were built.

Though regretting he was never able to visit Egypt, Dusty was a mine of information about the ancient world; architecture, building techniques, religions, migration of populations and all manner of other related topics. Quite why he never went into teaching or wrote books about his subjects escaped me for he was very well-read on them and more than willing, at least with me at any rate, to talk about them.

On a business trip to Egypt shortly afterwards I managed to make a lightning trip to the Serapeum at Saqqara, a place I had long wanted to see, and on my return I was questioned very closely by Dusty as to what I had seen and heard.

In brief, the Serapeum was built to accommodate the mummified remains of the sacred Apis Bulls and each was placed into huge stone sarcophagi in chapels off the main tunnels, each about the size of London Underground train tunnels, in the bedrock far below the sand.

The lids of the sarcophagi fit their bases perfectly and, to add to the mystery and wonder of the place, the height of the chapels barely permit the lids of the sarcophagi to be raised, let alone to allow the placement of the mummified remains of the bulls into their bases with the lids raised. Even more wondrous is the fact that the bases of each sarcophagi are exactly slotted into holes in the rock and between which one cannot insert a knife blade.

On the face of it, there would seem to be no way in which the sarcophagi can be manipulated above their respective holes and then precisely lowered into them if the base and lid are both in position and, moreover, there isn't enough room to lift the lids and then insert the mummies of these huge bulls into the bases.

So that particular morning, Dusty and I had much to talk about as we discussed the obvious mystery of the underground Serapeum and the amazing tombs it contained. Dusty had his own theories and I heard much about them in the days and weeks following that discussion.

In essence, he believed that the ancients, not only in Egypt but also in other countries, had knowledge that is now lost and that they could manipulate stone and other heavy objects by means of sound or vibration. He was completely convinced that in some way the ancients were able to induce a form of weightlessness in such objects which then enabled them to be manipulated in ways that we cannot imagine.

In due course, our discussions moved on to the theory, very common these days, that there existed in extremely ancient times, prehistoric times, civilisations that were wiped out and their knowledge almost but not quite lost. Dusty was convinced that Atlantis and other great civilisations existed millennia before ancient Egypt, and he could point to a number of monumental structures around the world to support his theories.

Then one winter weekend, Dusty saw an advertisement for a heavily discounted holiday in Egypt and, putting Bess into local kennels for a week, off he went full of excitement that he was at last going to visit the country and the ruins that so inspired him.

I saw him a couple of weeks later, and never before had I seen him so animated on the subject of the Egyptians and their predecessors.

He had taken various tours taking in the pyramids, the Serapeum and many other monuments which he had explored for himself. His excited and gabbled account of what he had seen was not only interesting but it was astonishing how much detail the man had absorbed during his short visit.

Even more startling was his admission that he now knew the secret of how the pyramids were built and what their purpose was.

I believe myself to be reasonably intelligent but I understood not a word of Dusty's explanation as to why the pyramids were built, for he now spoke in almost mystical terms and, because of this, much of what he told me did not make a great deal of sense. The gist of it, as I now recall some years later, was that the pyramids were a channel for some form of cosmic energy which a civilisation before that of the ancient Egyptians utilised to control not only the weather and the climate but what he termed the 'life force' of the country and its people.

I don't subscribe to these sort of theories but, on the other hand, there can be no doubt that the ancient Egyptians, and many other ancient civilisations, possessed knowledge and skills that are lost to us in these supposed days of high technology. Anyone who has seen a television crew's attempts to build a pyramid (smaller than the capstone on the Great Pyramid), for example, would recognise the superiority of some ancient skills over that of the present day.

Dusty was only too happy to discuss the purpose of the pyramids and he quickly became boringly and obscurely eloquent on the subject.

But, when asked how the pyramids were built, Dusty became as mute as an Egyptian mummy itself. He simply would not be drawn on it at all and I soon learned not to raise it again.

In 1987 parts of Britain were devastated by a hurricane which felled trees and caused much damage around the country. In our area, the local councils cut up the felled trees and many of their remains found their way to a spot on Two Tree Island which eventually became known locally as the Tree Trunk Graveyard.

The sight of so many tree trunks, and particularly one that looked amazingly like the long neck and head of a prehistoric dinosaur sticking up from among them, drew much attention from those people enjoying the island. And one morning found Dusty and I admiring the various shapes which were now becoming clad with moss and plants and bemoaning the fact that a vandal had destroyed the dinosaur.

I mentioned to Dusty that it would be a great thing for the council to cut up a couple of the massive tree trunks and set them out as benches for people to enjoy.

'I could fix that if I wanted to,' he replied, 'it would have been no trouble at all to the ancient Egyptians.'

I forgot the boast until a couple of weeks later when, on a very misty autumn morning, Soda and I encountered Dusty and Bess walking towards us.

'I fixed it,' he said.

'Fixed what?' I asked.

'The bench. I took a nice log and put it out on the grass.'

It took a moment for this to sink in, and then I realised that he was claiming to have taken a tree trunk and had set it down somewhere for people to use as a bench.

I asked him to show me the site and we walked over to a spot close to the Tree Trunk Graveyard where a sizeable length of tree trunk had been laid out on the grass near the path.

I felt Dusty was pulling my leg. 'But the council could have done this!' I said.

'Come back in a few minutes,' he replied. 'Then you'll see.'

Soda and I continued along the path to where it started to curve and then retraced our steps through the swirling mist. As we walked back I thought I detected the faint sound of a short burst of humming, reminiscent of the low, bass chant of a Buddhist monk.

I could not believe what I now saw. The huge log, weighing perhaps half a ton or more, had in just a few minutes been placed on the other side of the path leaving an area of flattened, dying yellowed grass where the log had lain just a few minutes before. And at seven o'clock in the morning, there was not a council worker or machine in sight and, nor for that matter, were Dusty or Bess.

I saw Dusty the next morning. 'Now do you believe me?' he asked, and I had to admit that I did. I did, because I saw the evidence of his efforts with my own eyes and I accepted it because I had once witnessed something very strange for myself which involved a huge weight.

In that instance, I was travelling in India many years ago with a work colleague and was taken by our Bombay director to visit a tomb about ten miles from Poona where, it was said, the spirit of a dead holy man would respond to a prayer and allow five men to toss a heavy stone ball high up into the air with as much ease as if it had been an giant football. My colleague and I were sceptical but nonetheless expressed an interest in seeing this phenomenon but not understanding that we would be invited to participate in this apparent miracle.

We arrived at the tomb and were taught to chant a few words in Urdu. Outside the tomb was a huge stone ball, whose weight I could not possibly guess since I doubt that three men could have lifted the thing. Despite this, I joined four local men and was instructed to place an index finger under the stone and, having uttered the phrase in unison with the others, toss the ball into the air. To my absolute astonishment the ball flew high into the air, perhaps, fifteen feet or so, and came thudding back down again into the position it had just left.

My colleague next tried the same thing with the same result and I have the photograph of the event to prove it. But how to explain it, that is quite another thing.

Here now, looking at a heavy log that was not in the same position as it was a few minutes before, I had no option but to admit that the act had taken place for the evidence was sitting there before me. But how Dusty achieved it, will always remain a mystery. Dusty would not discuss what had happened and positively refused to repeat his amazing feat.

He died a short time afterwards taking the secret of the ancient Egyptians with him to the grave.

Another secret to which only Two Tree Island itself knows the answer.

Sixteen ~ A Posh Old Gentleman

A short, tubby jovial man with white whiskers *a la* Santa Claus and a cut-glass accent that suggested good breeding, Bill Richards, or to give him his correct honorific, Captain William Richards, was eccentric by any standard, though completely and utterly harmless.

Bill was a lovely and exceptionally polite old gentleman, a posh old gentleman in fact, but he came as a bit of a surprise to those who didn't know him when he greeted them with a definitely nautical, 'Ahoy there!' And, since Bill imagined himself to be on the bridge of an ocean-going ship at all hours of the day and night, his conversation was more than likely to be liberally peppered with maritime terms. So, for example - and ignoring the fact that the bearings he gave were only relevant to his own position and not necessarily to those of the people he was addressing - if he spotted a rain shower coming in over the estuary to his front and right he might report, 'There's a squall coming in on the starboard bow!'

The effect was heightened somewhat by the commands he gave to his Skye Terrier, Jack. 'Belay that, Jack! Come for'ard where I can see you!' or, 'Tack to port, Jack!' As the long-suffering Jack was more than slightly deaf, and Bill had to raise his voice to be heard by the animal, passers-by often looked round to see if a ship commanded by a manic, drunken skipper was about to run aground on the salt marsh.

I met him a few years ago and, since I was involved with ships all my working life, had a natural affinity for the old sea-dog and, perhaps, took less notice of old and familiar maritime terms than did other non-nautical types.

There was one hilarious occasion when, after having a slight collision with a car being carelessly driven out of the car park down on Two Tree Island, he was explaining the circumstances to a baffled policeman who happened past in his patrol car a few minutes afterwards. 'I was in the fairway doing around ten knots when this yachtie tried to cut across my bows, rammed me on my port quarter and stove me bulkhead in!'

The explanation in such nautical terms was beyond the experience of the young police officer and, as the other driver was clearly at fault and had readily accepted the blame for what was in reality only slight damage, the officer wearily put his note book away and went on about his business pretending he had seen and heard nothing.

Bill was a former passenger ship master with a mine of stories, and I suppose that it was inevitable that on the occasions we met on Two Tree we would walk together around the metalled path as well as along Memory Lane, for there is nothing more calculated to bring instant happiness to those like me with a shipping background than a touch of nostalgia about the 'old days.'

Bill was a lifelong bachelor and was never more happy than when at sea; spells of shore leave were merely boring interludes to be patiently suffered while waiting for the next posting. Ultimately he had to retire on grounds of age and, though he did a couple of cruises in the early days of retirement, his pension was limited and these brief trips had to be curtailed.

But the sea lived on in his mind which was exceptionally sharp, except for his eccentric use of shipboard language, which as I have said oftentimes took people unawares.

Tales of navigation before the days of satellites and GPS receivers, and entry into port before the introduction of radar, of rich and famous passengers travelling to and from the mystical east were meat and drink to me, and Bill was only too delighted to pass these yarns on to anyone who expressed a remotest interest in them.

My walks were occasionally enlivened by Bill's stories. One of his ships had loaded ammunition at the explosives anchorage at Chapman's Reach out in the estuary not far from Two Tree, and Bill's description of landlubberly officials climbing a rope ladder up and down the tall side of a heaving cargo ship in a rough sea from the deck of a small boat was side-splitting, though I assume not to the poor devils involved.

Bill had adventures all round the Far East and could reel off the names of bars and restaurants in which many of these had occurred; indeed, a couple of these places were familiar to me even though my own visits could definitely be considered as pedestrian compared with his.

Clearly, Bill enjoyed the finer things in life and even he had to admit that it was a wonder sometimes that his alcoholic intake on such occasions never seemed to impair his ability as a ship's captain. 'A hair of the tail of the dog that bit you, along with an old-fashioned English breakfast with all the trimmings, is the only real answer to a hangover, old boy!' he often averred.

I heard tales of titled ladies seeking favours, sexual and otherwise, from their cabin stewards and captains on the long runs out to India, of ship's doctors who were quite, quite mad and rarely seen outside their cabins during the voyages, of crew members selling the ship's brass-work and anything else of value that might be detachable at the ports along the way, of the extraordinarily disgusting habits of some ship's cooks in his early days on cargo ships, and of some of the cargoes that were sometimes carried.

But, now I come to think about it, the vast majority of Bill's stories were about parties and the people that attended them. Drinking sessions on board his ship or on board the ships of other companies or on visiting naval ships. Drunken runs ashore and heavy parties in embassies and consulates, sessions in bars and restaurants and even the better class of brothel. Tales of seemingly harmless but nonetheless amusing alcoholic sessions in just about every part and port of the world one can imagine and especially in those places that prohibited the consumption of alcohol. 'Stolen fruits are always the best, old boy!' Bill insisted, waving his walking stick in the air to emphasise the point.

And then one warm spring afternoon, and Bill was yarning to a young lady whose small child was sitting on a fence, holding the lead of a puppy in one hand and slurping at an ice cream held in the other.

The puppy saw something of interest and dashed off to investigate it, and the little girl was suddenly pulled backwards off the fence. As she landed on the grass, she started to choke on some ice cream that had been forced down her throat.

I wasn't there, but I heard later from Bill that the young woman went into hysterics and was frozen to the spot while her little daughter struggled on the ground to get her breath.

Bill stepped in immediately, pulled the girl up into a sitting position and gave her a sharp thwack on the back. The ice cream slipped out of the girl's throat and she quickly recovered. From what Bill told me, the little girl recovered more swiftly than did her 'utterly useless, hysterical, landlubberly clot of a mother.'

Clearly Bill had saved the day and, thanks to the initiative of one of the folk who were close to the action and saw it for themselves, Bill was shortly afterwards honoured as a hero and featured on the front page of one of our local newspapers.

Alas, it was his undoing.

One of the paper's readers had moved to our area from London not long before and recognised Bill immediately. And about two weeks later, it came out in the same newspaper that Captain William Richards was, in fact, none other than one Harry Davis who used to be a butcher in Dalston and had never been to sea, not even on a cross-Channel ferry let alone a cruise ship.

It was all very sad and Bill, as I much prefer to remember him, disappeared from that moment.

How Bill acquired his vast and detailed knowledge of the sea can only be imagined but, for him and the people he yarned with, it was all very real and also very interesting. I am sure also from the conversations we had, that Bill's love of the sea was quite genuine even if he wasn't. Whatever way in which he obtained his knowledge and the background to the experiences he passed on must have required much research, for I and a number of others who spoke with him from time to time never found anything in his stories to suggest that he was a fraud.

In truth, it didn't matter to me for I liked Bill immensely; he fitted the part of an old sea-dog perfectly and his tales were very amusing, sometimes informative and always uplifting to someone like me.

But, of course, people do not simply disappear completely for they pop up somewhere else, sometimes in a different guise.

So I hope that Captain William Richards has appeared in another place, hopefully in another version of my beloved Two Tree Island within sight of the sea, and that he is carrying on in his old, totally and utterly harmless, way and giving enjoyment and the occasional surprise to the people that he meets along the way.

And I hope also that this posh old gentleman, if he ever reads this tribute to him, will avoid like the plague any small child sitting on a fence with a dog leash in one hand and an ice cream in the other!

Seventeen ~ Go Home!

Over the years I have met a variety of folk - some normal, some decidedly odd - with strange theories, though none of them ever seemed to prove or accomplish much either with their individual talents or their ideas, although Dusty Miller (see Chapter Fifteen) was a most notable exception.

I have a chum, for example, who will not mind me saying that he is a dab hand with a dowsing rod but who has never actually proved that the water he supposedly detects with it is actually under the ground that he never digs up. I once met a chap who believed he could locate gold deposits by passing a pendulum slowly over a map; that he never actually discovered any gold didn't seem to concern him in the least.

One person I knew was a firm believer in ley lines, those mysterious and usually invisible lines that seem to connect ancient sites for reasons which are obscure to say the least. I often had much fun with this chap when I used to point out the various coincidences which connected, for instance, the end of Southend Pier (built in 1890 and extended and improved a number of times subsequently) to at least seven highly important and ancient religious sites within a hundred miles radius.

Did the builders of Southend Pier deliberately factor into their ground plans, the pier head's relationship to a variety of sacred sites? I didn't think so, and my point that you could make almost anything appear to be related to something else, however unrelated or nonsensical, simply by drawing lines on a map went completely over his head.

But one person who was commonsense personified was the Reverend Mike Ball, an old chum of mine, and when one winter morning he called me for some advice, I was more than a little intrigued.

Thanks to a spell of very cold weather, the world bore a crisp white mantle of snow that Monday morning and I was about to take Soda out for a walk when the telephone rang. 'Are you going down to the island this morning?' Mike asked. 'Because, if so, I would like some advice.'

Since I had never been asked to give advice to a clergyman before, I was fascinated to know what sort of advice he might want from an old cynic like me.

Mike had retired from a living in the Midlands and moved back to his Essex birthplace where he occasionally helped out with baptisms, weddings and funerals or, as he called them, 'Hatches, Matches and Dispatches.'

The biggest problem in Mike's life was his chronic absent-mindedness and I often heard about the latest tale of woe that had beset him. Such as the morning he cleaned his teeth with hair gel, or the day that I found him walking awkwardly and learned, with much ribald amusement on my part I have to admit, that he had mistakenly rubbed a muscle-ache cream on his piles instead of an equally well-known brand of haemorrhoid ointment. 'Fair bought tears to my eyes, did that!' he exclaimed without any embarrassment. 'That'll teach me to wear my reading glasses more often!'

I put a thick coat on Soda and, well-wrapped up against the cold, we headed down to Two Tree Island where we waited in the warmth of the car for Mike to arrive with his black Scotty, Jock.

We didn't have long to wait on a freezing morning where, above a clear blue sky, a weak sun shone in the east and was counterbalanced by the faint orb of the moon in the west. Between them could be seen two aircraft glinting in the sun, their white contrails thickening and fading behind them.

Mike arrived shortly and we set off along the sea wall at the edge of the reserve. Soda ambled off with her mate Jock leaving Mike and I to take a closer look at the birds that could be seen that morning. There was much to see.

The tide was fully out and the wading birds could be seen foraging in the channels around the salt marsh. On some of the raised portions of the marsh various birds could be seen huddled with their heads in their wings as protection against the cold;

the colours of some seemed to blend with the thin layer of snow. Far out on the mud flats hundreds of Brent geese could be seen milling around and heard noisily squabbling with each other as they jockeyed for position or for food.

On the reservoir were half a dozen ducks aimlessly floating on the green water. Around the margins three moorhens scavenged between the reeds. A little further on a heron stood motionless in the shallows and suddenly jabbed at a tiny fish which it threw slightly into the air, expertly caught and then swallowed before returning to its statuesque pose.

A large owl was perched on an old pole sticking out of the mud of the salt marsh and was being subjected to feint attacks by three squawking gulls. The owl took not the slightest bit of notice of the gulls which were just feet away from it, but its head slowly swivelled to follow the progress of the dogs and Mike and myself as we moved towards and then away from it at about twenty yards distant.

Mike, who is extremely knowledgeable about birds and who can usually be relied upon to answer any question I might have on the many types that can be seen on and around the island, identified the bird as a barn owl which he thought was probably in transit somewhere and had stopped off for a bit of a rest.

We stood and watched the bird for a while, amazed that it took no notice at all of the screeching gulls which continued to make feint attacks around the huge bird. Eventually, it got bored with the birds' unwanted attention and flew off in the direction of Leigh Church, the gulls pulling back in alarm at its sudden movement.

Mike didn't seem anxious to tell me why he had wanted to see me that morning but it was clear that his interest for once was not in the birds.

'So why did you want to see me?' I eventually asked with much curiosity, and Mike pulled out of his coat pocket a large polished black pebble through which ran a brilliant white streak of some other type of rock.

'What do you think of that?' he asked.

There isn't much that you can say about a large polished black pebble with a white streak running through it. 'It's pretty,' I responded cautiously. 'Where did you get it?'

The tale was fairly simple to relate but not so simple to understand.

Mike had conducted evensong the previous evening at one of the local churches and a member of the congregation had asked to meet with him afterwards. The man explained that he and his wife had taken a holiday in Hawaii a couple of years before and had bought this pebble home as a souvenir of one of the historic sites he had visited. Since bringing it back, he and his family had been the victims of an extraordinary run of bad luck in which the poor fellow and his wife had fallen sick on a number of occasions, he had gone bankrupt and they had lost their house. To cap it all, his wife had left him. He blamed all this and a string of other strange occurrences on the pebble and asked Mike if he would exorcise the stone and then have it returned to Hawaii for him.

Having listened to the man and seen his very obvious distress Mike agreed to help even though he could not believe that an inanimate object could harbour evil or affect someone's life.

'You've travelled the world a bit. So what do you think?' he asked me.

As I have said, in my time I have met all sorts of oddballs who have strange theories and this one seemed decidedly odd; if the tale was true then all the people who collect stones when they visit beaches or ancient sites would have bought down all sorts of problems on their heads afterwards. Indeed, there is a large pebble in my garden that I once bought back from a visit to Cornwall many years ago and half a dozen potsherds from Egypt and Jordan lying forgotten around the house somewhere and none of these seem to have caused any harm to my household. Could such objects dislike being moved and take revenge? I doubted it. On the other hand, the man who Mike had met clearly thought that this particular pebble was hexing him in some way and so, perhaps, there was a logic in sending it back to where it came from.

Mike agreed. 'It could only be nonsense, of course. I understand that. But on the other hand ...'

'You're a clergyman and supposed to know about these sorts of things. What do you mean, 'On the other hand,'?' I asked.

'If you had come home with me last night, you'd have understood,' he responded.

To the immense and very tangible relief of the man in church, Mike had taken the stone, blessed it and had promised to send it back to Hawaii.

Mike got back home from church at about nine o'clock the previous evening. Within half an hour, four light-bulbs in the house had burned out, then his kettle shorted itself when he went to make a cup of tea and, finally, he smelt burning coming from his television set and he immediately switched it off and unplugged it from the mains.

'How do you account for all that?' he asked.

Absent more information about the electrical wiring of Mike's house, I couldn't of course.

I could only say what I would have done in Mike's shoes, and that was to tell the stone that it was going to be sent back home, and then to pop it in a padded envelope and ship it straight back to Hawaii.

And that is exactly what Mike did. He went home, told the stone that he was sending it back to its home, put it in a padded envelope and sent it back to Hawaii by airmail within the very next hour.

Hopefully about a week later, the Chief of Police in Honolulu received a polished black stone with a white streak running through it from a retired Anglican clergyman who politely asked for the stone to be returned to the site from where it had been collected. It solved Mike's immediate problems and, so far as he ever discovered, those of the man who disturbed it as well.

But it didn't help with Mike's chronic absent-mindedness. For a little while later I learned that he had once again mistakenly and very painfully applied a well-known muscle-ache cream to quite the wrong part of his anatomy!

Eighteen ~ Happy Christmas!

Christmas is undoubtedly my favourite time of the year.

I love the general atmosphere, the carols, the decorated streets and shops, and the universal feeling of goodwill and eager anticipation. People seem to soften and are cheerier than normal and despite whatever the government of the day has been up to in the previous weeks. Children look forward to the season - and their presents - with excitement and there is an air of festiveness around. Indeed, it appears to me that folk are far more likely to exchange greetings to strangers at this time of year than at any other.

We were about a week away from Christmas when one Saturday afternoon just after a late lunch Soda, Judy and I took a walk round the park on Two Tree Island.

We were well wrapped up against the cold and, since the sun had not managed to penetrate the cloud layer during the day, the heavy overnight hoarfrost remained on the ground giving the illusion of a light snow fall, and leading to the thought that perhaps we might have a white Christmas for once (though we didn't!).

Despite the cold there were a number of people to be seen out and about, some couples with their dogs and two joggers wearing, as they always seem to, the look of people in extreme pain. In the middle distance was a lone cyclist doing his best with the limited facilities on Two Tree to put his mountain bike through its paces.

We took the park path towards the hard where the rigging of the boats snapped noisily against the masts and where the wind blasted through the gaps in the hedge and ruffled Soda's tail. Soda could not bear her tail being interfered with and she stopped to see who or what was teasing her, and I paused momentarily to watch her puzzled expression as she tried to identify this invisible force. Judy stopped also but for no other reason than I had come to a standstill and so she stood there watching me while I watched Soda.

It was a fortuitous stop, for a short distance away and held in the thin branches of a skeletal bush was the most beautiful spider's web clearly delineated in all its detail by the frost. The spider itself was nowhere to be seen but its web was simply staggering in its design and construction and, though I am no photographer, I was sorry that I did not have a camera with me to record this marvel.

I bent down to take a closer look at the web and could not find a single fault with it. It was just perfect, as if it had been made moments before and then blast-frozen like a bag of garden peas. Nothing was missing and every strand was of the same thickness. Every ring was exactly symmetrical and each was joined to the other by stays that were regularly and evenly spaced. The whole was perfectly tensioned and suspended at even points by threads of differing lengths dependent upon the distance from the web to the branches of the bush around it.

I usually pay no attention to spiders' webs but this particular one on that particular afternoon was a wonder to behold and it seemed to me to represent Nature's own Christmas decoration. The grasses, bushes and the trees were all covered with a white crust of hoarfrost and all seemed to me at that moment to be saying 'Happy Christmas!'

Am I a romantic? Possibly, but the sight of that spider's web and a world covered with frost just seemed to fit the coming festival.

We wandered on past the Sea Scout hut and were warmly greeted by a couple walking their terrier.

Soda is definitely a ladies' dog and, ignoring the terrier, immediately ran up to the woman, squatted on her rump and put up a paw in the certain anticipation that her own style of greeting would lead to some fussing and petting. Which, of course, it did.

'She'll put up with hours of that!' I warned and the couple laughed, wished us a Happy Christmas and then went off towards the park entrance and the shelter of their car. I had not seen this couple before and the Christmas spirit was with them in their happiness and their willingness to greet a perfect stranger, even one with a dog that could spot a likely soft touch for some petting a mile off.

We crossed over to the path by the sea wall and walked along that for a little while. The tide was turning and the few boats that remained moored in midstream were swinging slowly on their moorings. The half dozen or so gulls that were to be seen were squatting low in a desultory fashion on clumps of exposed marsh and trying to avoid the biting wind. An unseen plane took off from Southend Airport and flew noisily overhead.

As the path rejoined the main one, the two red-faced, panting joggers came round on their second pass and called out 'Happy Christmas!' I was tempted to ask them why, if jogging caused them so much pain, did they carry on doing it, but this seemed against the spirit of the moment and I cheerfully returned their seasonal greeting.

Judy stopped to investigate a scent she had detected on a clump of grass by the side of the path and Soda, ever inquisitive, wandered over to check it out for herself. Leaving Judy to conduct a more thorough investigation, Soda bounced onwards.

Unless you are going to divert for a walk around the Lagoon, the path now swings towards Leigh Creek and runs back through the centre of the island.

Here we came across George, a beautiful sleek Dalmatian, and his mum and we stopped briefly, me to enquire about George's health and Soda and Judy to greet their old chum in the usual doggy fashion. For once, a petting was not on Soda's mind.

'Happy Christmas!'

'And a Happy Christmas to you too!'

Close to the Tree Trunk Graveyard, we were overtaken by the chap on his mountain bike. Gasping great clouds of steam he called out, 'Happy Christmas!' as he shot off towards the car park.

It seemed to me that his back wheel was slightly wobbly, possibly as a result of a collision with one of the pieces of hardcore or metal that are embedded in the ground off the main paths. If that was so, it didn't seem to affect his Christmas spirit one bit judging from the cheery tone in his voice.

Now our walk was almost done and we came to an open area close to the park entrance. This is the point at which I normally put the dogs back on their leads so as to avoid any accidents as we cross over the road into the car park.

Most drivers are mindful of the people, children and dogs that are likely to be crossing the road, but there are always exceptions to the rule and on Two Tree they are frequently caused by youngsters driving their Escorts as if they were competing at Brands Hatch. Therefore, caution is always best exercised when crossing the road with dogs.

I had not noticed them before, as they were tucked away by a mound on my left-hand side which gave a little protection from the wind, but to my astonishment there was a young couple with two small children in the last stages of having a picnic. Heavily muffled against the weather, they sat at benches by the picnic table on which was laid out a chequered tablecloth containing the remains of the meal that they had just enjoyed along with a small candle guttering in a glass container.

And this on a freezing cold day with a wind keen enough to slice bread and with the darkening sky bearing the certain promise of pending nightfall.

As often happened when Soda spotted people having a picnic, she immediately shot off to investigate and promptly shoved her head into a wickerwork basket by the side of the table to see what goodies might still be inside. Judy also knew when there might be a snack available and she shot off at her own pace after Soda.

The two children were delighted with the dogs' sudden arrival, and they were soon being fussed and cosseted and given a treat of some sort by the parents.

I was embarrassed both by the sight of people having a picnic on such a bitterly cold day and also because of Soda's insatiable curiosity, not to say appetite, and Judy's unaccustomed doggy solidarity. I went over and put the dogs back on their leads and apologised for their intrusion.

'Buon Natale!' said the husband.

I have very few words of Italian but I was able to respond. 'Buon Natale é felice anno nuovo!' I said, gratefully pulling the words out of the deepest recesses of my mind and hoping that my pronunciation was half-reasonable.

My response came as a huge surprise to this charming Italian couple who had eccentrically decided to have a late picnic lunch in the open air whatever the weather, and I was immediately invited to join them in a festive drink.

Thus it was that on a Saturday before Christmas, the seasons greetings were exchanged with various cheerful people on a freezing cold Two Tree Island which itself seemed to be decorated in celebration of the coming festive season.

Including one set of greetings in which one or two (maybe three!) very fine glasses of ice-cold grappa did more to warm me up than did the heater of my car when I climbed back into it twenty minutes later.

'Judy'

Nineteen ~ A Shift In Time

Ignoring Southend Pier stretching out into the Thames Estuary in the far distance and a couple of blocks of flats spoiling the middle ground, the immediate views from Two Tree Island are dominated in the east by the tower of St Clement's Church above Old Leigh and in the west by Hadleigh Castle sitting astride the Downs.

The 15th century St Clement's Church, with its imposing watch tower, stands sentinel over Leigh Creek which is said to have been much used by local smugglers in former times. Indeed, the churchyard contains a tabletop tomb bearing the scars made when the revenue men and press gangs were said to have used it to sharpen their cutlasses in anticipation of trouble.

But it is Hadleigh Castle which most people notice from the island. Built in the 13th century, the castle fortress occupies a prominent position on the Downs and those that take the trouble to visit it will see for themselves the panoramic views that its situation affords across the estuary.

Built of Kentish ragstone, there is not a great deal of the castle left these days since much of the stone was robbed out over the years by local builders; indeed, repairs have recently been made to the castle to prevent its collapse.

From the island one gets a good view of the southeast tower which, from that viewpoint, looks more or less intact. Only when one visits the castle itself can one see that most of the interior walls are missing and that the southern section of the site has been destroyed by subsidence. John Constable painted the castle in the 18th century and it is clear from his painting that parts of the castle which existed in his time have since either collapsed or been removed for building works.

Nonetheless, the castle and its grounds are still interesting to visit and, as I say, they dominate the western view from Two Tree.

It has often struck me how the castle's creamy-grey Kentish ragstone takes on different colours to suit the weather or the time of day and, for this reason, I often look up at it as I walk the park.

On grey, wet days the castle walls take on a chilling darkness, a reminder of what was quite probably a depressing place to anyone detained there in olden times. On sunny days the walls positively shine with a golden brightness, turning to a pink or reddish glow on those rare occasions when we are treated to an almost tropical sunset.

It is about a couple of those wonderful sunsets and their possible impact on the castle that this tale is about.

Susan Moore was a retired secretary and her pride and joy was her beagle, Maude, who was probably just about the softest animal I have ever seen, excluding Soda and Judy of course.

Susan's hobby was painting in water-colours and she was remarkably talented at this, exhibiting some of her best pieces in local art shops and many of these were also featured regularly in Leigh's annual Art Trail.

With a placid disposition matching that of her dog, Susan was a delight to talk to about painting and art in general.

So it was with some surprise that one evening, as late summer slowly turned to autumn and gave us a memorable crimson sunset, that I came across a very distraught Susan who was hastening away from the field next to the golf range with Maude in hot pursuit.

On seeing me Susan slowed right down and, though no-one else was around but thinking that she might have been accosted by someone, I went over to meet her and see what on earth the matter was.

She was extremely upset and it took some time before she calmed down enough to explain what had happened, and only after I agreed to put my mobile phone back in my pocket and not call the police.

Her tale was, frankly speaking, a strange one but strongly reminiscent of the two ladies who in 1901 believed they had stepped back in time while visiting the park of the Petite Trianon in Versailles and who claimed to have experienced the sights and sounds of an age long past.

Susan had been sitting at her easel on the edge of the field and painting the castle and the sunset behind it when, as she explained it, she became very heavy-headed and slightly dizzy. She put down her brush and palette and reached down for a small bottle of mineral water from which she took a sip.

The feeling of heaviness gradually passed off and she picked up her brush and palette to resume painting once again. But imagine her shock when she looked up at the castle and saw it not as it appears now but as it was when it was first built.

The castle she saw had a number of towers and coloured pennants were fluttering from two of them. The sound of what she thought were men's voices drifted down to her and people could be seen walking in both directions along the path atop the Downs. There was a vague recollection of some shacks or houses close by the southern wall of the castle.

Susan fainted with the shock of the sight, and it was only when Maude gave her a concerned lick across her face that she came to her senses and ran back to where she met up with me in the car park.

In truth I didn't know what to think as I walked back along the field to collect Susan's easel and bits and pieces while she sat in her car and rested. Recognising that something was amiss, Soda stayed to keep the puzzled Maude company.

The castle as I saw it at that moment looked as normal as it ever did; in ruins and bathed in the crimson light of the burgeoning sunset. There were some modern houses in the distance behind it, as usual, and there were no people walking the path across the Downs. There was not a sound to be heard other than that of a passing train on the nearby railway line.

Susan recovered quite quickly and drove home and I put the incident out of my mind.

That is, until four days later.

Soda's chief joy when we first got her was chasing balls, and I sometimes took her down to the field by the golf range to play in the days before we discovered she had a heart problem and was only allowed to have gentle exercise. On this evening, I took her beloved ball with us and was throwing it short distances and her pleasure in retrieving it was evident.

This particular evening there was another superb sunset, and I was enjoying the sight of its gradual development while Soda chased her ball short distances, bought it back and barked for me to throw it again.

In truth, the sunset was a memorable one.

The sun radiated a golden glow that lit the castle walls with a beautiful pink tint. The blue sky became deeper in colour and slowly took on a crimson hue that gave the walls a reddish tint. The crimson gradually darkened to a deep red and the lights of Canvey Island began to appear.

It was then that I spotted my old chum Peter Hawksworth out with his dog, Fred.

Peter was an accountant in one of the local council offices and I had known him for some years. A down to earth and affable man from Lincolnshire, Peter's hobby was church architecture and he was a mine of information about Essex churches and their graveyards. If you wanted to know anything about the history of England, then Peter was your man and he would wax lyrical about how English churchyards were a mirror of English history.

I wandered over and saw that Peter was deeply engrossed in watching the sun as it set behind the castle.

'Do you see it?' he asked.
   'Yes, it's beautiful,' I responded.
   'No, not the sunset. The castle. Can't you see it?'
   'See what?' I queried.

I was amazed with what I heard, for Peter described a castle that I could not see and I remember the remaining few hairs that

I have on my otherwise bald head started to rise.

Peter saw the castle as Susan had seen it four nights before, though with his trained eye he appeared to be seeing much more.

The castle had five round towers at the end of high battlement walls and two of the towers had pennants flying from their tops. A gothic archway in the eastern wall was flanked by a row of wooden dwelling houses or shops. Of the subsidence that occurred many years ago by the southern wall there was not a trace, and Peter noted that the ground by that part of the castle continued out for some distance and that a few small buildings stood there also.

Peter described the faint sounds of music and jollification coming from the centre of the castle and also what he thought sounded like the clash of steel against steel, though he did not get any impression as to whether this was a blacksmith's noise or the sounds of sword practice; he thought possibly the latter as he heard what he thought was the sound of cheering from time to time.

As was the case with Susan, the path cresting the Downs seemed busy with people but Peter also got the impression of movement along the southern battlement.

Peter described the scene in front of us. I saw ploughed fields and a railway line, but he saw marshland intersected by a channel leading from the Creek to the foot of the Downs. A short wooden pier ran out into this channel and men were unloading a small sailing craft with various barrels and boxes and other men were carrying small barrels up a path leading from the pier to the castle.

That was the substance of what Peter described to me up to the point where he put a hand to his head and said he had a splitting headache and the vision apparently dissolved in front of him and normality resumed.

'That was utterly amazing!' he said and, though I had not seen what he had seen, his commentary almost bought me into the vision with him, so convincing was his narration.

Peter and I have discussed what happened that night many

times since. He has not been able to add anything to his original description except that he had the impression of smoke coming from the area of the southwest tower which he thought might have been the smoke from a kitchen.

I mentioned Peter's vision to Susan one morning a few days afterwards but, alas, Susan was so unsettled by what she saw that she did not want to talk about it again and has not done so since. It is a great pity for I would have loved to have got the two together and made a comparison of what they each saw.

Oftentimes in the evening I continue to look up towards the castle and wonder at the mechanism, if such exists, that enabled two people to see a vision of the castle as it once was.

And I often wonder too why it was that on that beautiful evening that Peter saw this vision, I was not permitted to see it as well.

Twenty ~ It's For You!

Our beloved Soda ultimately joined her predecessors in the great parkland in the sky and for months we were without a canine companion. I couldn't stand it any longer and eventually after much searching, little half-pint Ollie joined the MacDonald family and many months later continues to delight us with his innocent exuberance and his antics.

All dogs, and cats I suppose, have their individual characters and quirks and Ollie is no exception to the rule.

Most of our dogs have been acquired from animal rescue centres and so their early character and habit forming experiences with their original owners have been hidden from us.

We would love to have known, for example, why Soda had such an overpowering hatred of foxes, why Judy seemed afraid of men other than Yours Truly and why Ben had such an affinity with cats that he would encourage ours, who were completely unfriendly to our other dogs, to groom him for hours on end. And why, when we walked in the woods, Piggy was always drawn to sniff at a particular empty badger set and ignore all the other interesting holes and tunnel entrances in the ground.

Max was irresistibly drawn to water and so began a habit of always having an old towel in the back of the car. Much later on this came in handy when Soda indulged in her occasional habit of fox-shit-slithering, her version we surmised of anointing herself with the canine version of Chanel Number Five. Piggy's big thing was his aggravatingly slow, thoughtful inspection and contemplation of every single blade of grass he came across. Judy never had any real quirks or habits as she decided that her sole purpose in the short life she had with us was to be just two steps behind me wherever I happened to be and wherever I happened to be going.

In Ollie's case, he just loves grass. The taller and denser the better. When we are out and about, Ollie has only to see a decent clump of grass and he is away at top speed only to disappear into the waving tresses of the green stuff.

He chases it, snatching at the odd strand as he tears past and scattering hundreds of crickets and grasshoppers along the way in the summer months. He bounces in it and on it, his back and tail surfacing above the green ocean from time to time. He runs round in circles in it and up and down in straight lines in it. He pretends to hunt in it, at first as if he is stalking a potential meal and then at speed as he goes in for the kill. He rolls over and over and down in it, sometimes coming perilously close to tumbling into water (which he positively hates with an intensity that is surprising to witness) when playing near one of the ponds. Sometimes he will just throw himself down in it, his little short legs waving in the air. Never have you ever seen an animal get so much fun and enjoyment from grass.

There was an early summer morning when we were out and about at a time when most sensible people were still in their beds. No-one else was to be seen in the park and Ollie had his freedom but keeping me always in sight. This particular morning I was enjoying the peace of the park. The scents of the blossoms and early summer flowers were heavy on a slight breeze, birds were singing from their various habitats and the empty estuary was calm and reflecting the clear blue sky above.

I was also enjoying watching Ollie play in the grass. The fun he was having was infectious and I was musing as to what character he might be pretending to be today. Was he the Bloodhound of Bodmin Moor this morning, tracking down the scent of a fleeing felon? Or was he pretending to be the Wolf of the Wyoming Wildlands hunting his breakfast through the waving grasses?

And then, almost hidden from view but with the tip of his quivering tail showing slightly among the grass, he stopped. And barked.

I walked over to take a look at what he had found and there, by a flat stone, was a fairly new grey mobile phone. Ollie had found it and he was now guarding it, his long tail whisking furiously from side to side.

I picked the phone up and switched it on. The battery was completely charged and the phone ready to use, though a security code prevented this. I opened the back and saw the owner's name - Nigel - and his local telephone number neatly written in black ink on the battery. I called the number on my own mobile phone and a lady with a terrifically theatrical manner answered. 'Is Nigel there?' I enquired. But no, Nigel had gone off to work and the lady gave me her address, and as this was on my way home, I promised to call in and drop the phone off when Ollie and I had finished our walk.

We carried on with our walk, and Ollie carried on enjoying himself in the grass until I spotted one of his girlfriends, a lovely young black Labrador named Minnie, coming towards us in the distance who he rushed up to and played with for a while while I chatted with her owner. We met a number of other people as we strolled back and Ollie, always the most friendly dog in the world, had to stop and greet them and their dogs, be fussed, admired and discussed before allowing us to continue. So it was some time later that we climbed into the car and headed home via the house where Nigel lived.

We soon found ourselves in a tree-lined road outside a typical semi-detached house with a slightly overgrown front garden. As I climbed out of the car a curtain in a front window twitched slightly. We had been spotted. As I reached the front door, it opened a tiny crack.

'How terribly, terribly kind of you to return Nigel's phone. He will be utterly distraught to know he's lost it,' the effusive and theatrical, yet invisible, voice cried.

'It's absolutely no trouble,' I responded and I proffered the mislaid phone.

The door closed and a few moments later was opened again, this time slightly wider when an arm produced a magnum of champagne and waved it at me. 'You must have gone to a lot of trouble to find us,' she said. 'You really must accept this as a very, very small token of our very sincere and very appreciative thanks!'

'That's kind,' I said, 'but it's no trouble at all,' and when the bottle was waved vigourously at me once again I plonked the phone down on the doorstep and fled.

It takes all sorts to make a world, of course, but this invisible and over the top lady was an original in my book and offering me a magnum of champagne for the return of an inexpensive mobile phone did seem definitely over the top to me. As it also seemed to my wife when I later mentioned it.

Besides which it did seem odd to me that, since the phone had obviously been dropped some time the day before, the careless Nigel must already known that he had lost it and not mentioned it to his invisible wife. So how could he possibly be distraught when he must already have known it was gone? I forgave the wife for being invisible as I assumed she might not yet have had the time to get dressed; we had been out and about rather early in the day, after all.

Matters of the moment took precedence over matters of the past and I forgot all about the careless Nigel, his missing mobile phone, his distinctly odd and invisible wife and their apparent penchant for magnums of champagne.

Until the next day when Ollie and I were again out and about early on a lovely sunny morning when all was well with the world and we had the park to ourselves. Ollie was once again jumping and leaping around in the long grass having a whale of a time. And once again he stopped, and barked for my attention.

We had reached the same spot and there, by the same flat stone in among the long grass was that same bloody mobile phone. I left it alone. Evidently, the careless Nigel wasn't as careless as I had first thought. It was obvious to a blind man that the phone had been placed there deliberately.

Ollie and I kept that phone under observation for a few days. Ollie made a point of looking for it and barking to let me know when he found it. It was always there, but never replaced in exactly the same position. Always placed by the flat stone but with slight differences. I made sure of that, for I moved it myself a couple of times.

The business remained a mystery to me until one morning I saw in the distance a young lady with a small dachshund suddenly turn to look around and then move slightly off the path and pick something up from the ground. Sure enough, when we got to the spot a few minutes later the phone had gone. But it was back there again next morning.

How odd. Why would anyone hide a mobile phone in the grass to be possibly picked up by a dog or other animal or be damaged by the dew? If it was left there deliberately for someone to use, as certainly seemed to be the case, what was the point in it being replaced each time? I will never know the answer unless the devious Nigel reads this and satisfies my curiosity.

My wife's explanation is that the devious Nigel was conducting some form of clandestine affair with the lady who we saw pick the phone up. But, if that was so, why didn't she keep the phone? Why did she need the phone in the first place and why didn't she alternatively use her own home or mobile phone to make her clandestine calls to the devious Nigel? Why did she need to keep putting the mobile back, and when did she put the phone back?

Perhaps only the long grass knows the answers to these questions.

And if that is the case, little Ollie is quite unable to pass the news on to me when he rolls and tumbles next time in its waving, green tresses.

'Ollie'

Twenty-one ~ Drip, Drip, Drip

I had what you might call a wet dream that night, but it was not the sort of dream that you might imagine reading this. I seldom dream, but if I do the memory of it disappears within seconds of waking. This was such a vivid one that it remains sharp in my memory even now quite a few years later.

I dreamt that my wife and I were on a large ship, a very old-fashioned ship. We were at dinner in a huge restaurant that vaguely resembled that of the first-class saloon on *Titanic* and I recall remarking to my wife that one didn't see waiters dressed in tails any more these days. The restaurant was quite busy though I don't recall whether there were any other passengers on our table, and I remember clearly that each course was served under a silver-plated cover that was lifted with some ceremony by the waiters as they laid the food before us.

We had an excellent dinner and afterwards we went for a walk on the wooden promenade deck. The ship was very peaceful and a number of people were enjoying a post-prandial stroll, one man I recall was puffing on an extremely large cigar that I thought was absurdly long. The passengers seemed to be dressed in the style of the 1930s and this did seem strange to me especially when one gentleman doffed his top hat as he and his wife walked past us.

The outside world was dark and had a green tinge to it, and I started to be troubled when I realised that I could not find the horizon or see the water over which I presumed our ship was passing. At a certain point a large shadow caused me to look up and I was astonished to see the dark shape of a ship's hull passing high overhead and silhouetted against what was clearly the surface of the water.

At this point I realised that my wife and I were passengers on a ship that had sunk, was lying upright on the sea bed and would never sail again. Perhaps we, and the others, were doomed to inhabit this sunken vessel for eternity and my partner gave me a comforting hug when the spoken thought worried me. We were, after all, ghostly passengers on this wreck.

With that thought, I woke up with a sudden start to find the rain lashing hard against the bedroom windows and the wind screaming through the eaves. A cup of coffee was most definitely needed that morning.

My usual morning routine is to get up between five and five-thirty and let Ollie out into the garden if he has a mind to rouse himself (which is not often, as he seems to like his bed!), make myself and my better half a hot drink and, while she enjoys a lie-in, sip my coffee in front of the idiot-box and get uptodate with the overnight news.

On this day the early television news bought us yet more doleful tales of problems with NHS waiting lists, lack of dentists, Iraq, Iran, possible rail strikes, failing school systems, juvenile obesity and the threat to tax 'unhealthy' foods, promises of punitive action and more fines against the long-suffering and overtaxed motorists for relatively trivial offences, etc., etc., etc. It was all so very depressing. There were government promises to fix this, that and just about everything else and all this regardless of its past track record which, to be fair, was probably not much different from any other recent government.

The news was just dreadful! Can't someone start up a *good* news channel?

To add to the misery of the day, a fierce gale was blowing in the outside world and at six-thirty Ollie and I set off for a very wet Two Tree Island. I still had my dream on my mind and the wetness of the day merely added to the general dolefulness of it.

We were soaked to the skin even before we had walked the short distance from the car park into the reserve. I drew the collars of my anorak closer together and Ollie put his nose down to the ground in an unsuccessful attempt to avoid the worst of the weather. Unsurprisingly, there were no other cars in the car park and no-one else was to be seen anywhere.

It was the year that the summer solstice fell on a chilly June day on which we switched our central heating system back on again. Three days later, on the so-called Midsummer Day, temperatures had plummeted even further and gales were blasting across our bit of East Anglia. Needless to say, Wimbledon had got off, once again, to a shaky start at least insofar as the weather was concerned and I wondered, as I do every year, why the organisers of this event arrange for it to take place at a time when rain seems almost guaranteed.

It really is no wonder at all that, barring our constant moans about the latest antics and ineptness of our non-achieving yet politically-correct, arrogant and spin-doctored, U-turning overlords, the state of the weather is the main topic of conversation of the long-suffering British people.

Since he seems to get involved with just about every minute aspect of our daily lives, I was considering writing to the man in charge to see if he would agree either to fix the weather or, alternatively, tell the people that regulate time that midsummer ought to be deferred for a month or so until global warming proper kicks in and we could enjoy decent weather. Then again perhaps he could call a series of meetings to sort the situation out or to have Wimbledon Fortnight deferred for a few weeks so as to save the players from freezing to death or from being drowned.

Whatever. You get the impression, I am sure, that on this particular morning - just a day after what was laughingly referred to by the television weather forecasters as Midsummer Day - the weather was more than just dreadful when Ollie and I set out for our morning walk.

And, maybe - just maybe - it was possible that I was not in the very best of moods as the wind loosened the collars of my jacket just enough to let the rain trickle down my back.

We entered the gate of the reserve and I checked out the latest list of birds that had been seen in it over the previous few days while Ollie found some temporary shelter behind a sodden bramble bush.

In truth the reserve looked bedraggled. The branches of the

trees and bushes as well as the taller grasses were bent over both by the wind and the weight of water on their leaves. I noticed that the branches of one bush sprang back slightly as the water fell to the ground and this action was repeated as the stinging wind and driving rain persisted.

The weather had caused its usual havoc. The access roads to the island and its car park were largely under water. Leaves and branches along with tiny fruit buds that had been torn off bushes and trees by the high winds lay scattered across the paths. Long grasses had been flattened in some places by the heavy gusts, and it was curious how the wind seemed to have selected certain areas for flattening and not others. One could see that the water in the reserve's main pond had been raised to one side by the force of the wind and sodden, drowned plants now hung limply over its edge. There were no birds to be seen anywhere and the rabbits sensibly stayed in their, presumably, dry burrows.

It really was not a good start to the day.

Ollie growled irritably, blinked and shook his head as a droplet of water dripped off a leaf and, shattering on the tip of his nose, spattered into his eyes, and we carried on walking to the end of the main path to where he would normally have jumped up onto a log for me to sit awhile and give him some petting and attention. But not this morning; the pair of us were soaked through and our only thought was to get back to the car and out of the way of the biting wind and the rain.

Back along the path, Ollie and I diverted to the left where a large open space gives access to the path running alongside the reservoir. We would not take that path this morning but the space gives open views to the estuary and I had earlier spotted the bows of a heavily-laden container ship going up river towards Tilbury docks and which were burying themselves now and again in the battered whitecap-covered waters, and I diverted briefly to take a closer look.

The ship and its spume-scattering movements were an impressive sight, and I was reminded of a hurricane I was once involved in many years ago when I saw from a ship's bridge her huge forecastle disappear under the green and angry foamy seas.

It was the only time I was truly seasick and the memory of that awful morning and the hours of misery that resulted came flooding back to me now.

People sometimes talk about the 'real sea' and I briefly mused as to what this meant; the term is surely relative. What seem to be real seas to someone standing on the bridge of the container ship I was now watching, must be horrifying to someone cowering in the cockpit of a small sailing boat. And, perhaps, what seem to be real seas to someone in a small fishing boat may seem to be relatively calm waters to the helmsman of a large ocean-going vessel. Whatever the relativity of the term that came into my mind, one thing was certain and that was the seas out in the Estuary that morning would be extremely dangerous to anyone in a small boat.

I was interrupted in my damp nautical reminiscences by the faint sound of what seemed to be a whimper and Ollie shot off to my right to take a look for himself, searching various areas before finally settling at one spot where he stopped and enthusiastically wagged his tail. I walked over to where he was now dancing around a large clump of dripping teasels and saw he was getting excited at a small rabbit trying desperately to make itself invisible among the thicket.

Closer inspection showed that what he had found was not a rabbit but, in fact, a small, cowering, and very wet and distressed Yorkshire terrier that was clearly now terrified it would be harmed by the noisy and excited Ollie and his large dripping owner.

I picked up the shivering and soaked little creature and it offered no resistance. Once cradled in my arms and, hearing some soothing sounds, it gave me a lick from a tiny mouth and thoughts of dear little Judy came flooding back into my mind.

We walked quickly back to the empty car park where Ollie jumped into the back and patiently waited for me to dry off this little creature before I gave him some attention. The Yorkie quickly perked up and the two animals sniffed each other before curling up on Ollie's imitation lambs-wool blanket.

Where had this little Yorkie bitch come from, who and where was its owner and how long had it been lost? Its tag did not show its name but did give a local telephone number which I immediately called on my mobile phone. There was no answer; possibly the owner was even now out looking for the animal.

In the few minutes or so it had taken me to dry the two dogs off, the windows of the car misted over completely and I started the engine and switched the airconditioning on for a little while to clear the fog.

There were still no other cars to be seen in the car park and no-one else seen to be walking in the park. We had encountered no-one in the reserve and so that was ruled out as a place where someone may have been looking.

There was nothing else for it but to go and look round the other side of the park and, leaving the dogs in the car, I set off once again in the wind and rain to check. A brisk, if wet and cold, walk proved fifteen minutes later that I had been alone.

That left the sea wall on the southern side of the golf range, the playing field on its northern edge and the fields running alongside the road by the railway line.

I started by checking out the sea wall; nothing. Apart from a deliriously happy Labrador and its wet and dejected owner, there was nothing to be seen on the playing field.

Climbing back into the car, I drove slowly in the direction of Leigh Station; there was nothing to be seen in the open spaces opposite the railway line.

Except for the newspaper distributors that gather by the council refuse tip with their vans early every morning, there was nothing to be seen and I was beginning to wonder if the little dog that Ollie had found would become a member of the Clan MacDonald and I was not unhappy at the prospect. Already I could hear slurping sounds coming from the back of the car and I guessed that Ollie was giving his new friend a wash.

But it was not to be, for just past the vans and walking along the sea wall was a young woman, head down against the driving wind and rain and seemingly on her own. Was this the missing owner?

I turned the car round and parked it. 'Have you lost a dog?' I shouted against the screaming wind and her nod confirmed that she had.

I climbed out and the woman came down from the sea wall and looked into the back of my car. 'That's my Henry!' she exclaimed with evident relief.

'Henry?' I asked. 'This dog's a bitch!'

'It's short for Henrietta,' the woman explained, and on hearing her voice the little Yorkie stood on its hind legs and its stumpy tail started to wag furiously.

So that was it, my momentary dream of giving Ollie a new companion had come to nought.

But we had reunited a lovely little animal with her very relieved owner who, she told me, had lost the dog the previous evening when she had scampered off after spotting a bird in the car park. I was glad Henrietta had survived an atrocious night and perhaps because of the weather that might have dissuaded foxes or other dogs from doing the little creature any harm. The evidence of a joyful reunion was there before my eyes and I was glad of that. Ollie was none too happy to be parted from his new friend though he is always delighted to meet her on the odd occasions we see her and her owner on summer afternoons.

And I have to say that, once indoors and relaxing in dry clothes after a hot shower, I did feel that we had achieved something that miserable, wet and windy morning and that all was reasonably well with the world.

And this despite the soggy dream that started the day - and despite the so-called midsummer weather and the antics and ineptness of our non-achieving yet politically-correct, arrogant and spin-doctored, U-turning overlords!

Twenty-two ~ Enough Already!

No matter what the weather is doing, it usually occurs to me as I turn past Leigh-on-Sea Station in the mornings to cross the railway line onto Two Tree Island that the long-suffering commuters almost always look completely fed-up, and there is no doubt that sometimes they have very good reason for this.

Complaining about British railways is, along with gripes about the government and the state of the weather, a national pastime. Where else but in Britain do the railways come to a standstill at the slightest hint of snow or the fall of autumn leaves, rails buckle in summer heat or overhead power cables collapse in high winds? How is it that the Scandinavian and Baltic countries manage to carry on in the depths of their Arctic winters and the Mediterranean countries manage to run their rail systems in the hottest of summers? When one considers - as I used often to when travelling on what we here call the Misery Line - what some of our European neighbours have to contend with in terms of extremes of weather, running a railway line in this country would, on the face of it at any rate, seem simple by comparison.

At the time when Ollie and I usually pass by the station in the morning the number of folk heading for the trains is not great, but on the occasions when I see people milling around the forecourt I know instantly that something has gone wrong with the system and that, by the time we have finished our walk, there will be crowds of commuters trying to get buses to other stations or phoning their wives to come back and collect them. These mingle with people just arriving who, seeing that there is a problem, immediately jump back into their buses, cars or taxis or trudge wearily back up the hill towards Leigh.

It is on mornings such as this that I offer up a silent prayer of thanks that I no longer have to face the twice-daily trauma - for trauma it truly is - of the commuter struggle to and from London.

On this summer morning the sun was already beating hot in a

cloudless blue sky and the song birds were singing their hearts out when Ollie and I left the house. A fox languidly crossed the road in front of us and slipped into the garden of our next door neighbour; Ollie regarded it as another friendly breed of dog and merely wagged his tail at its passing. At the bottom of our road a woodpecker was running along the gutter picking off insects as it went along; a form of fast food for birds I thought to myself, as I have now seen this odd sight many times.

As I came to turn by the side of Leigh Station a number of commuters were milling around outside. Clearly the trains had conked out yet again or else the overhead lines had come down or a rail buckled or something, and my cheerfulness was slightly, only very slightly, tempered in a gesture of sympathy for them.

I headed towards the railway bridge and, as I did so, I was forced to slam on the brakes when a red-faced, shirt-sleeved commuter suddenly dashed across the road in front of the car and waved his fist furiously at a train that was standing on the Chalkwell side of the station. I don't think the chap saw me at all, though as I was doing no great speed, no harm was done but his anger and frustration was very evident not only to me but to the startled people around him.

Ollie and I had a great walk in the reserve.

Ollie was in one of his stocktaking moods and was checking, as it seemed, every blade of grass and stem of bush to see what might have changed since we had strolled past them the previous evening. His nose quivered appreciatively at one of the fence posts and I wondered what scent he had registered and whether it was rabbit, fox or dog or even something else; alas, he could not tell me. As it happened, a slower walk that morning suited me just fine for I was enjoying the wild flowers.

Bearing in mind that much of the island is the result of accumulated rubbish and spoil, the range of flowers is sometimes quite surprising. As the year progresses one sees plants that have obviously been included in people's garden rubbish and which have taken root in their new surroundings; tulips, daffodils, hyacinths and roses of all different types and colours are to be seen growing haphazardly among the fruit trees, bushes and scrub.

I don't know what the difference is between a weed and a flower (please don't bother writing to tell me!) but in summertime they all appear the same to me and are part of the magic of Two Tree. Buttercups and daisies proliferate along with dandelions, saxifrage, cow parsley, various types of ferns and grasses and these are all mixed with lords-and-ladies, primroses, harebells, honeysuckle, bindweeds, wood-sorrels, dog-roses and all manner of other plants. Some of these I assume have been blown on to the island, such as for example the fast-spreading rape, and others included in the spoil that has been tipped on to it.

Whatever the origin of the plants, they make a lovely show during the year and it is a delight to see what has sprung up from month to month. I look forward to the spring flowers, including the bluebells on a little patch which includes clumps of white albino ones and, in summer, I especially enjoy seeing the delicately coloured sweetpea.

Ollie and I had a pleasant and very gentle walk and, because no-one else was around to divert his attention, straying not very far from me.

We stopped at the end of the reserve and sat on the log there, Ollie enjoying his morning petting and me drinking in the views of the Estuary, of Old Leigh and of the castle. The only sound was that of a cockle-boat's engine puttering away in Benfleet Creek and of an aircraft passing high overhead. The absence of any sound coming from the railway line reminded me that it seemed to have come to a standstill.

It was time to head back to the car and then home and, perhaps, we walked a little slower on the way back because of the sun's increased heat.

Back in the car I started the engine and switched the airconditioning on, luxuriating in the cool air as it built up and expelled the hot air of the car's interior. After a few minutes, we pulled out of the car park and headed back towards the little bridge over Leigh Creek.

It was there that I spotted the chap who earlier I saw angrily waving a fist at the stationery train by the station. He was standing on the middle of the bridge with his shirtsleeves now rolled up and with his necktie gone. He was twirling his briefcase round his head and then, almost as I drew level with him, he threw it into the creek.

I pulled to a halt, wound the window down and asked him if he was OK. 'Never felt better in my life!' he said smilingly and so Ollie and I took him literally at face value and left him happily watching his briefcase float down the creek on the outgoing tide. And I did wonder if this particular commuter hadn't just decided that it was too much stress and effort and given it all up.

When we breasted Leigh Station the forecourt was, as I had anticipated, crowded with hot and angry people all milling around and trying to decide how they were going to get themselves to London without a train service.

Poor devils I thought and, offering another prayer of thanks that I am no longer part of such a stressful pantomime, threaded the car slowly through the crowd and headed off up the hill towards home and breakfast.

Two weeks later Ollie and I were again walking the reserve, only this time Ollie was in a hurry to greet one of his chums he could see further along the path. He first met Holly, a Labrador puppy younger than himself, about a month before when he heard her owner calling her name. Thinking that she was calling his name Ollie got excited and, as he does when he doesn't get his way instantly when he wants to say hello to another dog, screamed as only he can. People who know us now ignore his screaming tantrums but I do get glared at from time to time when others think that my little half-pint friend is being mistreated.

Anyhow, this morning he was anxious to get to say *hi!* to Holly and the first bit of our walk was brisker than usual until we had met up and the canine greetings had been properly exchanged. Once that was done, Holly and her owner turned to walk back along the sea wall by the reservoir while Ollie and I carried on along the main path.

A boisterous young border collie bitch, unusually tan-coloured and very pretty, appeared out of nowhere and squatted down with wagging tail to wait for us to come up to her. Ollie was delighted to make a new friend and the two nuzzled each other and were evidently friends immediately. When the dog put a paw up for me to give her some fussing, I knew that I had made another new friend as well.

Presently the dog's owner came along and I recognised him immediately as the chap who had chucked his briefcase off the bridge on the day the railway line came to a standstill.

'Didn't I see you throwing your briefcase into the creek the other day? I asked him.

'Too right!' he said. 'I'd had enough of the whole damned business!'

John's story might be familiar to some people. He had worked in a dreary office for an ambitious bully of a boss who had no thought or regard for his staff who he demanded work long hours for poor pay. Even worse, John strongly suspected his boss of having his finger in the till and of sacking junior staff to cover up his misdeeds. I heard also the familiar tale of uncomfortable trains that didn't often keep to time, that were cancelled or replaced with shorter carriage sets, of overcrowding and the awfulness of being jammed into impossibly overcrowded Underground trains especially on hot summer days.

John's descriptions of the travelling conditions and the daily grind in an oppressive office bought the whole thing clearly into my mind, so when I saw him reach boiling point that morning and then chuck his briefcase into the creek in a final gesture against the awfulness of his position, I understood immediately and sympathised with him totally.

John did not remember waving his fist at the stationary train, but he did recall deciding that he needed to take a walk and cool off before he did something very stupid. And in the mile that he slowly walked between the station and the little bridge over Benfleet Creek, he decided that none of the stress and aggravation he was suffering was worth the salary he was getting. The act of throwing his briefcase into the creek, which incidentally contained an important report that his boss was going to present to his own superior that morning (but which he would not now read), not only effectively terminated his employment but symbolised a new beginning for him.

Of course, there are many more people like John who would like to chuck it all in and stay at home but there are not many, like him, that have a small pension to fall back on. And, perhaps, there are not many who would subsequently fill their days totally absorbed in a hobby. In John's case, it is nature; he is an absolute whizz with trees, plants, birds and animals and is a fascinating man to talk to.

I see John and his lovely dog, Bonnie, now and again when Ollie and I stroll the reserve of an afternoon or evening (not everyone wants to get up at sparrow's crack like me!) and I am always happy to pick up a new titbit of information.

Which is how I came to know the difference between a damselfly and a dragonfly, and how little half-pint Ollie came to love and adore Bonnie.[2]

But that is another story.

---

[2] When resting, a damselfly folds its wings along its body, whereas a dragonfly keeps its wings outstretched (like a parked aircraft).

Epilogue

It was high summer and Ollie and I had gone down to the reserve on Two Tree Island just before the sun rose in an attempt to avoid the heat of the day.

No-one else was around at that early hour and Ollie looked around in vain to see if any of his mates were in sight; alas, they were not and the little half-pint was stuck with just me for company.

Ollie is such a social creature, we are thinking of finding him a companion. In the meantime, he has built up a coterie of chums that are almost all female and with whom he tears around each day. His best friend is my sister's lurcher, Nell, and she is followed next in popularity by Minnie, a young black Labrador, and then by our neighbour's dog, Barney. In order of preference after that come Lucy, a lovely sleek greyhound owned by another neighbour of ours, Molly, another young black Labrador ... and many others that he loves to chase and play with. Indeed, there was one memorable morning when eight dog owners and eleven dogs peacefully walked the park paths with the dogs all getting on wonderfully with each other.

So, on this morning, little Ollie stopped and wistfully looked back at the gate to the reserve to see if any of his chums might be following and then, realising that they were not, he resigned himself to walking just with me.

We had a gentle walk in perfect peace with only the bird song for background noise. There had been a little dew and this had encouraged the slugs which seem only to inhabit one part of the reserve by the entrance and are rarely seen further east except where the creatures have some grass over which to slither.

A gentle breeze wafted in from the estuary bringing with it the faint scent of cockleshells mixed with that of the wild flowers and, as the sun rose, the crimson, cloudless sky lightened into a wonderful uniform shade of blue which was reflected in the mirror-like calm of the full-tide estuary.

A blackbird was singing to his mate and, possibly sensing that we were no danger to him this morning, didn't bother to call out a warning on this occasion. Gulls floated quietly on the waters surrounding the salt marsh. Two swallows circled above us, causing Ollie to stop and take an inquisitive look at what might be causing a shadow to cross his path. A grazing rabbit seeing us approach languidly lolloped off into a bush, starting up the resident pheasant which blundered noisily off towards better cover.

The blackberry bushes were in full production and it would not be long before the fruit pickers arrived to harvest these and the apples that would go into the pies that would result from their labours. The elderberries, faintly scented with a hint of the liquid to come, also waited for the winemakers to come and stock up on the ripening fruit. In a while, the pears would be ripe for the picking also.

Butterflies fluttered about the teasels and the brambles and, for once, the midges had taken the morning off, perhaps it was yet too early in the day for them.

It was one of those summer mornings which got progressively hotter as the sun rose, and before long I was wondering whether it had been such a good idea to come out at daybreak when, perhaps, an earlier start under the light of the full moon might have been cooler for both of us. Even Ollie didn't have the energy this morning to run and roll around in the grass.

We had got to the eastern end of the reserve and Ollie had clambered up onto a log in readiness for me to come up and give him his usual bit of petting and grooming while I surveyed the scene.

The air and the views were as clear as crystal, and the coast of Kent looked so close you thought you might be able to reach out in front of you and grab a chunk of it.

To the northwest, the main tower of Hadleigh Castle was lit with a reassuring, timeless golden glow. The Downs were covered in lush grass and the cornfields beneath them showed where the combine harvester still had work to do. To the east, the flag on the tower of St. Clement's church hung limply at the masthead.

It was high tide and the waters of the estuary were as calm as they ever could possibly be. There was placid water stretching out to the east beyond Southend Pier for as far as the eye could see and, apart from the gulls floating lazily on its still surface, there was no movement at all and not a ship or sail boat in sight. An invisible curlew called from the salt marsh and was answered by a quack from an unseen duck on one of the ponds.

Around the edges of the salt marsh the mauve tips of the sea lavender bent slowly to and fro, and I wondered whether the samphire that I could see in one place would make good eating and whether or not it would be worth the effort of crossing the mud at low tide to get to it.

We retraced our steps a little way and then turned off to return by way of the sea wall and the reservoir.

Ollie stopped to look down into the dirty water and peered disapprovingly at the ducks and moorhens that were searching the margins for their breakfasts. His ears pricked up at the sound of a gentle 'plop' where a water vole or rat had dived into the water, and though we both looked hard, we could not see the animal, if such it was, that had caused the sound to reappear.

Watching Ollie peer intently at the spot where the widening ripples now spread over the surface of the water, I was reminded of one of his predecessors, Max, who one morning at around this time of year many years ago also heard a sound and went off to investigate it.

On that day, we were walking at the western end of the park and around the Lagoon, which at that time happened to be completely covered in a thick layer of bright green algae. Max heard a noise, looked up to see where it came from, decided that it came from the other side of what he thought was a field and set off at high speed to find out what it was all about. He never reached his destination for, to his utter astonishment, the lush green field he thought he was about to race across turned out to be plant-covered water and he plunged straight in.

People who are not dog owners insist that dogs have no expression, whereas any dog owner will tell you immediately that they most definitely do. We can tell, by the shape of the mouth, the position of the tail, the look in a dog's eyes and the way the ears have moved what a dog's mood is and, sometimes, what it might be thinking.

Max most certainly had an expression that particular morning for I saw the look of surprise on his face turn to one of irritation as he climbed dripping out of the water, shook himself and then discovered that he had become covered in a bright green layer of plant life. Not only that, but he stank to high heaven as well. It was one of the few times when Max actually seemed to enjoy a bath when we later got home, for algae and smell were both swiftly removed.

Thinking about Max inevitably bought to mind his successors; Ben, Piggy, Soda and Judy.[3] And of the many days they and I had enjoyed on Two Tree Island.

Lovely sunny high-summer days like this one, other days when the snow lay thick on the ground showing where the island's birds and animals had walked before us and yet still other days, wondrous, mysterious days, when the swirling, rolling fog and sea-mist were so thick that we could see only a few feet before us and when every muffled sound carried with it a slight hint of menace. There were many other days, of course, days when the spectacular sunrises or sunsets forced you to stop and admire them, days when the wind seemed sharp enough to cut right through you, days when the rain fell so hard that you were drenched within minutes and days when the ground was so muddy and slippery that you wished you had stayed on the metalled paths or even in bed.

All great days in their ways. And days on which I shared the

---

[3] Max, Piggy and Judy were acquired from private owners. Ben came from the Wood Green Animal Shelter of Godmanchester in Cambridgeshire (Tel: 08701 904090) and Soda and Ollie came from the South East Essex Animal Trust of Rayleigh in Essex (Tel: 01702 552951) - both organisations are very deserving of support.

furry and uncompromising companionship of my dogs.

But, standing now on the sea wall looking at the expression on Ollie's face, I could see that he was frustrated at not being able to discover the cause of the sound we had just heard. His ears moved back and forth like miniature radar dishes and his nose quivered as he fruitlessly tried to pick up a scent that would tell him what was going on.

Though Ollie and I have a close bond and can often understand each other's thoughts, I could only tell him that the vole or rat had taken itself home and would not be seen again while it was being watched. Perhaps he understood, for he lost interest at that moment. Each dog has his or her own personality; in Ben and Soda's case they would have hunted down the cause of that noise and spent an energetic half an hour doing it before giving up; Ollie, like Piggy before him, just didn't have the inclination or the energy and couldn't be bothered.

In any event, it was now time to head home. Besides which, it was getting very hot and both of us needed some shade and a drink.

The thought crossed my mind, influenced probably by the fact that on a hot summer's morning we were surrounded by water, that perhaps Two Tree would benefit from a water fountain strategically placed. But it was a silly thought, since the fountain would be expensive to install and be most likely vandalised within days of its installation.

As it happens, hidden away in the undergrowth where it can no longer be seen is the plinth of a Victorian water fountain produced by the Metropolitan Water Trough Association whose title is still to be seen on what remains of its marble column.

Doubtless part of the hard core and rubbish on which much of the island was constructed in the days when it was used as a rubbish tip, this fragment of a fountain was thoughtfully pulled up to the vertical by one of the people who helped to transform the tip into a park and nature reserve and now stands as a memorial to someone who, like me and many others, love the island and its peaceful walks.

It remains an interesting reminder of the days when goods were taken round the country by porters and horse-drawn carts at a time when philanthropists provided funds so that men and horses could get refreshment on days such as this.

But, alas, there is no water fountain on Two Tree and it was time for Ollie and I to head homewards, he to flop out for a rest on the settee in the living room and me to a reviving cup of coffee and a read of the morning newspaper.

It had been one of those peaceful, glorious mornings when one could truly say that God was in his heaven and all was well with the world.

Or at least that little bit of it that occupies Two Tree Island.

Leigh Marsh

What do these waving stands of grass
Know of the increased ozone about them,
Or the delicate pink dog-rose
Care about the trash buried beneath its roots?

What concern does the hawk have for the seeping methane
As it hovers above the cowering harvest mouse,
Or the ducks for the prismatic fluids
Streaking their tidal ponds?

My dogs trot around the man-made paths
Oblivious to the whining of the model aircraft,
As do I on a hot summer's day
When a cool breeze brings with it
The unmistakable scent of rotting cockleshells.